HER CHRISTMAS LIE

Racy Reunions Book 2

BY SYLVIA MCDANIEL

Books by Sylvia McDaniel

Contemporary Romance

Standalones
The Reluctant Santa
My Sister's Boyfriend
The Wanted Bride
The Relationship Coach
Her Christmas Lie
Secrets, Lies, and Online Dating
Paying for the Past
Cupid's Revenge

Anthologies
Kisses, Laughter & Love
Christmas with you

Collaborative Series

Magic, New Mexico
Touch of Decadence

Western Historicals

Standalones
A Hero's Heart
A Scarlet Bride
Second Chance Cowboy

The Cuvier Women
Wronged
Betrayed
Beguiled

Lipstick and Lead
Desperate
Deadly
Dangerous
Daring
Determined
Deceived

Scandalous Suffragettes
Abigail
Bella
Callie
Faith

The Burnett Brides
The Rancher Takes a Bride
The Outlaw Takes a Bride
The Marshal Takes a Bride
The Christmas Bride

Anthologies
Wild Western Women
Courting the West
Wild Western Women Ride Again

Collaborative Series

The Surprise Brides
Ethan

American Mail Order Brides
Katie

Her Christmas Lie
Published by Virtual Bookseller

Cover Design by RomCon
http://www.romcon.com/

Edited by Tina Winograd
www.tinaeditservices.com

Formatted by Laurelle Procter
laurelleprocter@gmail.com

Short Description: Tyler Ferguson shows up at Kelsey Johnson's door without any memory of breaking off their engagement.

ISBN: 978-1-942608-54-7 (paperback)
ISBN: 978-1-942608-07-3 (e-book)

{Contemporary Romance – Fiction}
{Holiday Romance – Fiction}

www.SylviaMcDaniel.com

Synopsis

Tyler Ferguson thought losing your memory had some advantages, but mainly it created problems. When a roadside bomb in Kabul exploded the Humvee he'd been riding in, and wiped his memory of the last nine months in Afghanistan, he'd been given a medical leave to come home just in time for Christmas. And Tyler is so excited to see his fiancée, Kelsey Johnson.

Kelsey can't believe it when she opens the door and there stands the man she still loves, but had broken off their engagement while he was deployed. Doubts of being able to live with Tyler in constant danger, of only seeing him several months a year had her ending the relationship. When she realizes he doesn't remember the breakup, she thinks that life has given her a second chance with the man she loves. At least until his memory returns.

Can a wedding and Christmas heal Tyler and give Kelsey the strength she needs to be a military wife? Can a soldier forgive the girl he loves when she sends him a Dear John letter?

Table of Contents

Chapter One

Losing his memory had some advantages, but mainly it created problems. Like how could he forget where Kelsey Johnson, his fiancée, lived? Of course, she'd moved here during the months he liked to call the dark days. He couldn't remember a thing from March to November because a roadside bomb in Kabul had obliterated his Humvee, giving him a near death experience and a one month hospital stay in Germany. All courtesy of Afghan insurgents.

Marine Second Lieutenant Tyler Ferguson shifted restlessly in the back seat of the cab. How would Kelsey react when she saw the bandage on his head and the wound in his leg, which was better, but far from healed? He'd been lucky. His driver, Sargent George McDonald didn't fare as well and he hated that. They'd become friends as he drove him around the desert rebuilding the infrastructure so his fellow marines could communicate and do recon work.

He'd been gone nine months, and for the last two, he'd had no communication with Kelsey. She must be worried sick. Him showing up unannounced, he hoped was a great surprise. He couldn't wait to gaze into her green eyes and let his fingers comb through her silken red curls.

Would it be rude, just to pick her up and carry her straight into the bedroom? He'd missed her so much; his heart ached as the miles separating them shrunk. It'd been so long since he'd felt her warm, loving arms around him.

Just the thought of seeing her, brought tears to his eyes. For a while he'd thought he'd never see her again. But finally his body had responded to the doctors' treatments and then they'd delivered the bad news.

Maybe he'd lost more than just days in a hospital. Maybe he'd lost months, possibly forever, but his mind was working, his body was healing and even his leg was better. He had a lot to be thankful for.

So he couldn't remember the last nine months. The blast seemed to sear away the time he'd been in Afghanistan and frankly, he was okay with that as long as he could remember today and yesterday and every day going forward. Especially if it was spent with the woman he loved.

Snow fell softly as they drove through the Denver, Colorado neighborhood. He'd found her address on Google and given it to the driver. The cab pulled to a stop and he gingerly stepped out, hoping his bad leg held. Paying the driver, he said, "Thanks, man."

"Good luck, soldier," the cab driver said.

Tyler felt a grin spread across his face. Yanking off his cap, he pulled out the Santa hat he'd bought in the airport. With flowers in one hand, his duffle bag in the other, he limped up the sidewalk to the front door.

The home looked inviting, a wide wooden porch, with patio chairs beneath the overhang eves. The neighborhood was an older, more settled type of homeowner. The kind of place with families and dogs and backyard barbecues. The only problem was Kelsey hadn't decorated for Christmas which surprised him. She loved the holiday season and always decked the house from the inside out.

With trembling fingers, he rang the bell and waited impatiently. Just when he was ready to give up, he heard the door locks being pulled back. Anticipation at seeing the woman he loved tore at his rapidly beating heart. This point in time seemed to drag clear into next week. When she pulled back the wooden door, he opened his arms wide. "Merry Christmas!"

For a moment, Kelsey stared at him in shock and then she came outside. Gently, she reached up and put her hand to his head. He'd waited so long for her loving touch...a whole four weeks, but he knew it'd been longer. "You're hurt."

"Yeah, I had a little meeting with a roadside bomb. But the insurgents didn't live to tell about the destruction they'd caused." The doctors had refused to let him remove the bandage around his head until after the next appointment.

"Tyler," she whispered her voice choked.

Why wasn't she kissing him? Sure, he probably looked worse than he felt, but since the day of the bombing, he'd dreamed about her lips moving against his.

"Are you badly injured?" she asked.

"A little memory loss." He laughed and shrugged, wanting only to kiss her. "I've been anticipating your mouth and all you want to talk about is how badly hurt I am?"

Sweeping her into his arms, he pulled her body in close to him. His lips came crashing down on hers in a kiss that he'd been waiting for. A kiss filled with promises of love and devotion and assurances of nights of mind-blowing sex. He craved some between the sheets action with his woman in a major way.

Her arms slowly wound around him, as she gave herself over to the demands of his mouth. He wanted her as close as he could get her without doing the tango right here on her porch, under the stars, while the neighbors watched.

She stepped out of his arms and stared at him, her emerald eyes shimmering with tears. "Come in, Tyler, we need to talk."

~

Kelsey Johnson, stared in disbelief as the man she'd loved, promised to marry and then dumped, while he was away at war, walked into her home. Since her Dear John letter in March, she'd dated nothing but one loser after another.

One guy was a serial dater. One had a prison record and another wanted her to quit her job, sell her house, and move to the holy land with him. She'd dated them all and always compared them to this man in uniform sitting before her.

She'd loved Tyler so much she'd grown anxious and unable to deal with him being in a foreign country, doing intelligence work in a war zone. Finally, unable to live with the thought of him dying, she'd broken off the engagement and sent him a letter saying she couldn't live like this.

And she'd regretted her actions almost immediately.

But why was he here and why wasn't he angry with her? Tyler was not a man who would easily give a woman a second chance. And he hadn't said a word about them breaking up?

"How did you get hurt?" she asked. The sight of this man standing on her porch had her chest aching with need and longing. Loving him had come easy until he'd gone away and she'd realized it would be months before she heard from him. It could be a year before she saw him again. He could die.

"The Humvee I was in hit a roadside bomb. At least that's what I've been told."

Her stomach clenched as nausea rolled through her. The very thing she'd feared could happen to him in Afghanistan had and now he was walking with a limp and a bandage peeked from beneath the Santa hat.

"Are you all right?" she asked, frightened at the thought of him dying from a bomb exploding in a car he was traveling in.

He laughed. "Well the leg is healing slowly. But the mind. The mind doesn't want to remember the last nine months in Afghanistan. Seems like the bomb just wiped that part of my brain clean, like a virus on a hard disk."

Her mouth dropped open and she almost choked as the realization of what had happened overwhelmed her. She started to cry and he immediately took her in his arms. "Hey, baby, I'm okay. We're together. There's no need for tears."

But they hadn't been together for months. Even now, they were supposed to be apart. And yet, he didn't...remember. To him she'd never turned chicken and bailed. She almost felt like she was given a second chance. A gift from the gods to get it right this time or lose him forever.

"I didn't know you were hurt," she said, shaking in his arms as he held her. His brothers wouldn't have told her, his mother was in an Alzheimer's unit and his father was dead.

Stunned at her unbelievable good luck, if you could call it that. "You could have died. I should have come to you."

No, they had broken up. But he didn't know that. He didn't remember that awful letter she regretted writing. He was here with her at this moment and she loved the way his arms felt around her.

He kissed the top of her head. "Sorry, honey, I was in a hospital in a location they don't reveal." He sighed. "I've got to sit down. I've been standing too long."

Quickly, she released him and helped him to her couch. "What happened to your leg?"

"A piece of the Humvee lodged in my shin. They removed it, but the damn tendon is slow to heal."

The thought of the amount of metal that must have been twisted or flying during that explosion had her cringing. He'd been lucky and she was so grateful he was back in her living room.

"Oh Tyler, this is what I feared," she said, tears rolling down her cheeks. While she'd been safe here, in America, teaching kindergarteners the alphabet, he'd been fighting for his life.

Pulling her into his arms on the couch, he said, "I'm going to be okay. The leg will heal. And if the brain thinks those nine months were so bad that I didn't need to remember them, it's okay. As long as I'm here and I recognize you, I'm good."

She swallowed and looked down. The good part of her said she should tell him the truth and be honest with him. But the lonely, crazy, single-cat woman said don't let him go. He's the best thing that ever happened to you. And so she listened to the needy woman who wanted him by her side.

"Where's your ring?"

The engagement ring. It was in her closet in a box where she'd put it with the intention of returning it to him when he came home. But now she needed and wanted that ring desperately. "It's in the bathroom where I was washing my hands when you rang the bell."

He nodded his head. "Do you mind if I stay here?"

She swallowed, knowing that would mean sex and the charade would continue. The two of them together. The idea of him in her lonely king size bed was more than she could withstand. "Of course. How long before they ship you back to the Middle East?"

"I don't know. Maybe never. They want me to see a neurologist before they'll put me back on active duty."

The idea of him seeing a specialist frightened her even more, but the thought of him behind a desk, here in the States, made her almost giddy. The very reason she'd written her letter, not being able to cope with the idea of him being hurt in that desert would be eradicated. And while she knew he wanted to return to active duty, she hoped he never went overseas again without her.

Look what the insurgent forces had already done to him. What if there was shrapnel lodged in his brain and that's why he still wore a bandage and the reason for his memory loss. What if he had to return to active duty in the next few months and leave her? Could she deal with his loss all over again?

What if he went back only this time he wasn't quite as lucky?

"How did you manage to live through such a terrible ordeal?"

"I had to get home to you," he said, and kissed her again.

Her heart wrenched in her chest as she returned his kiss with a fervor of her own, needing to feel his wounded body as close to hers as she could get him.

The man had grown up in a military family. When they met, he'd told her, someday he would retire from the United States Marine Corp, but until that day, his body and his mind belonged to the United States government. And when he'd been deployed, she'd tried to be tough, but watching him walk through airport security, knowing he was gone for a year, she'd grown weak. What if never saw him again?

And then when months went by and she hadn't heard from him, she'd worried he was rotting in some foreign jail or some crazy terrorist group had captured him and he would be the next Internet beheading. Fear consumed her and she'd written the letter in desperation thinking she could not live like this. The not knowing was eating her soul away.

Now here he was in her house, kissing her, her body responding, knowing if he ever regained his memory, he'd probably hate her even more.

They broke apart, her heart racing, her breath coming in short gasps, the center of her aching, needing, wanting this man.

"I would tell you that for nine months I've dreamed of this moment, but I can't remember."

She started to laugh, but a tear trickled down her cheek. His injury was working to her advantage and part of her was sad and part of her was elated. He was here in her home, wanting to make love to her and she craved that time spent in his arms more than she needed her next breath.

"I don't have any condoms," she said.

Knowing without a doubt that by staying with her, she'd find him in her bed. And that thought left her aching with need. After all, she'd intended to marry him.

He grinned. "I picked some up in the airport. I thought we might need a whole box before this week was through."

Smiling, she ducked her head. A whole box?

"Are you up to it?" she asked, wondering if his body had the strength and endurance to sustain him.

Booming deep male laughter surrounded her and she felt a trickle of need wound down her spine. "I've been up since before I stepped out of that cab. Lord, woman, I wish I could pick you up and carry you to the bedroom. But that would be a problem."

"I could always carry you," she said.

"Not happening. Take me to bed, honey."

Chapter Two

Taking his hand, she led him down the short hallway to her bedroom. Funny, when she'd moved in here, she'd been glad there were no memories of Tyler in this room and now, tonight, they would create new ones of the two of them locked in each other's arms. Whatever doubts she'd had were erased as she led him into her sanctuary. She'd made a huge mistake in ending their engagement and now she hoped he never learned the truth.

Though her concerns were still there. If he went away again, she knew those same fears would move into her mind and build a commune, where she would struggle with the dangers of him being so far away.

His lips crushed hers and his kiss was filled with desire, passion, and a thirst for living. From the instant she'd seen him standing on her front porch, she'd been thrust back into the past. When things were perfect between them.

Her robust soldier, a strong man who'd known his path in life from the moment she met him in college, seemed to be wandering lost in the desert of life. How could she turn him away? Living without him she'd begun to doubt what they had. She'd let fear rule her life and now she was praying that as much as she loved him, she didn't want him to regain his memory and realize while he'd been brave, she'd been a coward.

His mouth drank from her like she was a living fountain, as she unbuttoned his uniform coat. Finally their lips broke apart and he stared down at her. "Are you going to be okay seeing my injuries?"

"Are you still Tyler Ferguson?"

He chuckled. "Yeah, I'm still the same person inside this battered shell of a body."

"Then I'll be okay with your injuries. I just don't want to hurt you."

"Oh, Kelsey, I'm afraid of hurting you. I want you so bad," he said, pulling her T-shirt over her head and unsnapping her jeans. "I'm about to burst like a rocket."

Reaching up, she cupped his chin and stared into his eyes. Her big strong man needed reassurance and she would do whatever it took to make him feel assured of her love.

"We'll be okay. Maybe the first time will be fast and hard and the second time will be nice and slow," she whispered, placing her lips along his cheek.

Tyler needed her and she had to make up for her mistakes. Hopefully he'd never learn about what she'd done.

He chuckled as he nuzzled the curve of her neck and shoulder. "I've missed you so much."

"Are you sure about that?" she questioned. "After all, your memory is gone," she teased, trying to make light of a difficult situation.

"My heart knows that I've longed to see you and that's all that matters. My mind follows my heart."

Her chest exploded with pain at his words. He was giving her unconditional love and she'd run at the first sign of trouble. But this time she would be stronger. She would do better.

"Oh, honey," she said, and sighed with pleasure as she shucked his military coat and saw his shirt and undershirt, waiting for her to remove. "You're wrapped up tighter than a Christmas present under the tree."

She tried not to look at his wounds. The scratches, the deep bruises that she realized must be from the explosion, weeks after that horrible event. She didn't want to think about that frightening day that she hadn't been aware of. To think that she was living her life, while he hung precariously in the balance between life and death. She hated war. She hated the military.

Yet she loved Tyler and knew that life with him would always be a military life. He was a soldier, a tough guy who took charge and thought his mission in life was to protect his country.

"Standard operating procedure," he said, and trailed his tongue along her neck and shoulder area, sending tremors shivering through her.

"If you don't stop, I'll never get you undressed," she whispered, realizing how right this felt. Like the missing half of her had come home. How many times had they made love in the past and yet this time felt fresh and new and so very right.

With a gentle shove, he pushed her jeans down to the floor and then flipped her onto the bed.

"Tyler," she squeaked.

"Kelsey, no more talking. Just doing," he said.

Laying back on the bed, she watched him as he finished removing her pants, leaving her in her underwear. Slowly, he removed his tie, his shirt, and quickly shucked his perfectly creased pants.

When he was down to his underwear, she saw for the first time the red, angry scars on his leg. She wanted to kiss them, hoping to send healing vibes his way, but instead she kept her eyes focused on his face as he approached the bed. He didn't need to see her concern, her fear, or her distress at the sight of his injuries. He needed her love and support and she'd give him that and the moon, too, if she could.

"Kelsey, thinking of you kept me alive," he said, as he lowered himself between her legs.

Her heart clenched with pain as she realized what she'd done to him. How could she ever make it up to this man that she knew she still loved with all her being? In his darkest hour, she hadn't been there and now she would spend eternity knowing she'd deserted him while he was at war.

Hooking his fingers in her panties, he slipped them down her legs, kissing her navel, letting his tongue slide down her belly, kissing her center. A groan escaped her throat and she clenched the bed covers. "Tyler," she whispered throaty. "Your leg. Don't hurt yourself."

She should be taking him in her mouth. She should be honoring him and yet she knew he was thinking of her pleasure. He was putting her first and her chest almost burst with pain.

Guilt ate at her, filling her until she thought she would scream out the truth. And then he pulled her legs up onto his shoulders.

"Honey, I'm just fine. This is where I want to be."

He kissed the inside of her thigh. His mouth blazed a trail up her leg to the juncture between her legs. Lovingly he caressed her sending tremors racing through her body as he licked leisurely at the folds between her legs. "Oh, Tyler."

His tongue circled her clit bringing her right to the brink of an orgasm, before he backed off and then came at her again and again, shaking her gently, driving her insane with need for this gentle giant.

Placing his hand beneath her butt, he lifted her and angled his mouth at just the right height to thrust his tongue deep inside of her, devouring her hungrily. Clutching at his head, she held him there, moaning as the orgasm she'd been holding off overwhelmed and sent her over the edge. With a cry, she bucked against his mouth as her body filled with tingles that left her shaking.

"Hurry," she whispered.

In a daze, she watched as he kicked off his underwear, ripped open a condom and covered himself before sliding into her slick body. Breathing heavily they stared into each other's eyes, and she could feel his heart pounding inside his chest, reassuring her that he still lived. And then he shoved into her, thrusting hard.

"Kelsey, this is what I longed for."

"Tyler," she whispered, unable to talk as he moved within her, filling, completing her. How could she ever thought of living without him? With every thrust, he seemed to hit every nerve, every muscle, every stroke reaching her heart, filling it with love for this soldier.

Clinging to him she felt another orgasm rushing towards her like a bullet train. Urgency filled every breath as she clung to him. With every gasp they were in sync, they were one. And she could see from gazing into his eyes, that he felt the emotion just as much as she did.

Tears welled up and leaked from between her lids as she cried out as passion surged through them at the same time. Like fireworks on the Fourth of July, they both came and this time when they finished, he wrapped his arms around her and simply held her.

"I don't remember it being this good," he said quietly.

But she did. The memories came flooding back of how they'd spent hours together in each other's arms. Hours of teasing and tormenting each other, laughing and loving one another. Like a movie, the remembrances rushed back, bringing a barrage of tears she could no longer hold back.

~

"Baby," he said, wondering if he'd somehow injured her. "I didn't hurt you, did I?"

He wasn't the gentle lover he'd dreamed of being since he realized his injuries would send him home for a short time. Home to Kelsey and the life they loved.

"No," she whispered in the darkness.

"It's okay. I'm here and we're together." Emotion poured through him like sand in the desert, filling him. Being here beside her felt so right, so natural. This was where he belonged. Yet his job was in the Middle East. His mission to protect the United States government's interests was his top priority and he knew that.

"Oh, Tyler, I know, but it was so good..."

"That you're crying?" he questioned. "You could be crying because it was terrible or terrific. How is a man supposed to know?"

Playfully she slapped him on the arm. "It was great. Tonight brought back all the memories of us and how good we are together. Even I had forgotten. So you're not the only one with memory issues."

He rolled to his side and pulled her into his arms. "This feels so wonderful to be lying here in bed with you, in America, where I belong."

Sighing he relaxed against the woman whose face he'd feared he would forget. He'd forgotten nine months, who's to say he would lose the memory of Kelsey and everything they had. And yet here he was in her bed, in her arms feeling like this he'd come home. Not out in the desert wearing fifty pounds of gear while he repaired cable.

"I know you probably wrote to me, but I don't remember. Tell me what's going on in your life. We've talked about mine, but what about you?"

He felt her tense in his arms and wondered why she stiffened.

She laughed and kissed his chest. "Sara is getting married in less than two weeks. In fact, there's a couple's bridal shower tomorrow night that we should attend. I was going to go alone and now you can go with me."

A twinge rippled through him. Sara was marrying his best-friend Jared and while he was extremely happy and knew they were in love, the thought of being surrounded by people with a bandage still on his head and limping, made him nervous.

He didn't like people fawning all over him or having to explain the last nine months were just a big black hole. But this was an event that he knew Kelsey wouldn't want to miss and he just wanted to be with her, so he'd suck it up and attend.

"Okay," he said not exactly enthusiastic.

"Everyone will be thrilled to see you. And you were supposed to be in the wedding party."

For some reason the U.S. Government didn't care when his best friend was getting married. They granted leave but there were limits. Weddings were not considered top priority. Hell, some of his men had missed the birth of their children, so who was he to complain.

"Only if I could get leave, which was denied," he said, thinking how strange that he remembered some things but not others and how there was no logical connection to what his brain thought he should know.

When they first told him, he'd worried and strained trying to remember, but it was like there was a dark hole during those days. But how could a man just forget a certain amount of time?

"How's school?" he asked.

This was her third year of being a teacher and he wondered at how he could remember minute detail like that and not what happened a month ago. It never ceased to amaze him what his mind would let him know and what it shielded from him.

"My class this year is really a great bunch of rowdy kids that I'm enjoying teaching. Some want to learn, some couldn't care less and some kids just want to have fun. It's been an excellent year so far."

"Great. I know you struggled that first year."

For a moment, he was sorry he'd asked Kelsey about what was going on in her life. It made him realize what all he missed when he was deployed. While she was here, living day to day, teaching kindergarten, he'd been over in the desert trying to rebuild a country that he often thought didn't appreciate what they were doing for them. But his opinion didn't matter.

"I think all teachers do. You get out of college and then reality hits and life is not what you expected," she said, rubbing her hand on his chest.

Just the touch of her fingers on his skin, had him catching his breath. He'd missed her so much. It felt good to be lying here in her arms, talking like normal people, instead of fighting a war.

"The military is the same," he said, trying to remember. He'd hoped when he made it home, he'd relax and everything would come flooding back. All his memories would rush at him, like a sandstorm in the desert, but so far no luck.

"Day after tomorrow is the last day of school. We're having our school party and I think it would be great if you came up and talked to the kids. Seeing you in uniform would make such an impression on them."

"Sure, I'd love to talk to the kids about serving."

His job as a soldier was to protect and serve the United States and he loved what he did for a living. His father and even his grandfather had served time in the military and if he ever had a son, he hoped he would join as well. It was an honor to wear the uniform, regardless where they sent him, or what they required of him, he was proud to be a United States Marine.

Reaching up she kissed him. "I know that when you left, I was scared and frightened and literally terrified you wouldn't come home to me. But Tyler Ferguson I'm so proud of you and the man you are."

He kissed her forehead as they lay there, naked in her bed. Kelsey kept him grounded in the real world and his job was another dimension where evil often won and yet everyday they fought for good. "Tell me about the wedding. Are they ready for the big day?"

Part of him wished it was his wedding day. That he and Kelsey were the ones getting married on Christmas Eve. He'd like nothing better than to claim her as his.

"I think so. The invitations have been sent, everyone has their dress or their tux, the flowers have been ordered, the photographer, the wedding cake, the caterer, I mean we've been through the list a half dozen times. Sara has freaked out on me at least twice over the enormity of the day, but I think she's ready."

All women seemed to want a big wedding, but he hoped that he could convince Kelsey to keep theirs small. The thought of such a big affair was overwhelming, especially now.

"Why did they choose Christmas Eve as their date?"

"They met at a Christmas Eve party three years ago. He gave her the engagement ring on Christmas Eve and they just feel like it's a magical day for them."

Tyler thought of his best friend, Jared. They'd been friends since high school, gone through college and now he was the first one to take the next step, marriage.

But Tyler knew he and Kelsey wouldn't be far behind. And he could hardly wait to begin their life together, even though he knew that sooner or later the U.S. Marines would return him to duty. A top secret assignment, black ops, where he couldn't call home except when he was in a secure location, which would be almost never and his letters would go through a screening before he could read them or be sent to Kelsey. Anything in writing between them would be known by some geek in a department in the U.S. Marines.

He shivered and she turned his head to hers and kissed him on the mouth. Oh, how he'd missed being right here, in her bed, his arms holding her close, her lips making him harder than granite.

She released his mouth and he reluctantly let her go. There were some advantages to being injured.

"I'm so glad you're home."

For now he was here, celebrating life in her arms, loving her and wishing that this time could last forever, knowing that sooner or later he'd return to being a soldier.

She leaned into him, her breasts crushing against his chest. The nerves in his manhood tightened in acknowledgement. The time for talking was over. They still had a box of condoms that he knew was going to be put to good use tonight.

"Show me how much you've missed me."

"With pleasure, Tyler."

Chapter Three

Walking in the door to her sister's couple's shower, Jared was the first one to spot Tyler.

He jumped up and came running to his friend. "What the hell?"

He grabbed Tyler and squeezed him in a man hug. "I didn't think the Marines would let you go."

"They didn't," Tyler said quietly.

Jared's eyes lifted to the bandage on his head. "You okay?"

"I'll be right as rain soon," Tyler promised.

Kelsey glanced around at the couples attending her sister's wedding shower. Only two years apart, it was mutual friends they'd shared since college, plus Jared's friends. People who knew that they had separated. Would one of them be so brazen as to tell Tyler the truth? She hoped not.

"What happened," Jared asked, concern in his gaze.

"Roadside bomb."

When she could see that all the attention was getting to be too much, she rescued her handsome soldier.

"Honey, you haven't said hello to Sara," she said, and whisked him away.

"Thanks," he whispered. "I don't like to talk about what happened and how I can't remember."

"It's okay. You don't have to tell anyone," she said, her heart aching with how this injury had affected him. She was just starting to realize the pain he endured.

She'd awakened last night and he'd been gone from their bed. When she went in search of him, he was in the living room, walking, trying to ease the pain in his leg. Finally, she'd convinced him that a muscle relaxer would help his body heal, and he'd taken one and come back to bed.

Afterwards, she'd lain awake for hours wondering at her decision not to be honest with him, her heart breaking that he was injured. She had to be here for him. She couldn't walk away. He needed her. And she was quickly realizing how much she'd missed his sweet smile, his caring heart, and the way he loved her.

Walking up to her sister, she watched her sister's mouth drop open. "Sara, look who's home."

Her sister's eyes widened and she stared at him. "But I thought-"

Kelsey shook her head. "Yes, the military was not going to let him have leave to come to your wedding, but he was injured and now he's home for a while."

"Oh my God," Sara said, hugging him. "Are you okay?"

"I'm all right," he said, stepping out of her arms. "Just a little memory loss. But who needs to know what happened."

As they stood there, Kelsey could feel the tension radiating from Tyler and wondered if it was because of the injuries or just going away to war and coming home. It had to be hard to adjust to everyday life once again.

Sara gazed at him, her eyes staring at the bandage on his head. "I'm so glad you weren't injured more seriously and you're here. Jared will be so happy."

"I'm happy I'll get to see you two get shackled," he said.

Kelsey knew he was trying to deflect the conversation from talking about his injuries and she didn't want to talk about what was wrong before she had a private conversation with her sister.

Jared strode into the group. "Hey, man, how would you like to be my best man? My father stepped in when we thought you couldn't make it, but I'd be thrilled if you'd stand up with us."

"Are you sure your dad won't be disappointed?" he asked.

Kelsey could tell that he wanted to do it for Jared, but he wasn't all that excited. And she wondered if it was because of his injuries or the tension she could feel from him. What if he wasn't okay? What if his injuries were more than what he was telling her?

"I just hung up the phone and Dad said he'd be relieved if you took your spot back."

Tyler gave Jared a man hug. "I'm happy to be your best man. You'll have to return the favor when Kelsey and I finally tie the knot."

Kelsey watched her sister's eyes widen and she knew what she was thinking. And it wasn't good.

Sara grabbed her by the arm. "Come see the cake. Lauren got for the shower, it's beautiful."

Glancing at Tyler, she wanted to make certain he was okay before she ran off and left him. She didn't want to leave Tyler's side as she had this urge to protect her manly soldier, but knew her sister had questions. "I'll be right back. Are you okay?"

He laughed. "I'm fine."

Cringing inside at what she knew would not be a fun conversation, she let her sister pull her into the kitchen and then out into the garage where they could talk privately. As soon as the door shut behind them, Sara turned on her.

"What the hell are you doing? You broke up with him."

"And I've regretted it for the last six months. I made a mistake."

"What did Tyler say about you breaking up with him?"

She licked her lips nervously, knowing her sister would not be pleased with her actions. "His injuries caused him to lose his memory. He doesn't remember the letter."

"Dear God in Heaven, please tell me you told him." She stopped. "Wait, why doesn't he remember the letter?"

"I couldn't tell him."

Her sister cursed.

"The vehicle he was in hit a roadside bomb. He can't remember the last nine months. The entire time he was in Afghanistan."

How did she explain the utter look of desperation on a man's face who was injured and hurting? She'd never forget the expression on Tyler's face as long as she lived. Or the guilt that consumed her when she'd seen him.

Sara's face clenched with sorrow. "No wonder he looks like shit. I've never seen him so pale and gaunt."

Tyler was thinner than Kelsey remembered and he'd always been tan, but not now. And while last night not telling him the truth had seemed like such an easy way to reconcile a mistake, today, she wasn't so sure. How would he feel if he ever learned the truth? And what if he had to go back to war? Could she live with him being gone?

"How could I tell him the truth?" Kelsey said, her eyes brimming with tears. "He showed up on my doorstep, injured, thinking that things hadn't changed between us and well...I had to let him in. Is it wrong to hope that he never remembers that letter?"

Kelsey just wanted to safeguard him, let him heal and enjoy their time together. That's all she was asking for. After the holidays, then she would make some decisions as to what to tell him.

Sara's mouth dropped open, her blue eyes grew wide with disbelief. "Of course it's wrong. He came home thinking nothing had changed and you're pretending that everything is okay. Yes, it's deceitful. You need to be honest with him because if you don't and he gets his memory back, he's going to be so angry that I fear he would never forgive you."

"I can't. Not now. I just can't."

And she couldn't. There was no way she would break his heart again if at all possible. Hopefully, his memory loss would keep him right here in the states he'd never have to go to that godforsaken country again. They'd already injured him once, she was frightened of what would happen if they were given a second chance. And she was terrified, she couldn't deal with him leaving yet again.

"You're risking everything."

"I know. But how could I tell him when he showed up with a bandage on his head and limping. I knew I'd made a mistake and this just seems like I was given a second chance to right a wrong."

At this moment, she felt strong. There was no way she would give up this time with Tyler. Not for any reason or anyone, unless he was deployed again and then she wasn't quite so sure.

"And maybe you're right. Maybe this is a second chance, but a good relationship doesn't have secrets. This is a really bad secret. Even if his memory never returns, you'll always have this between you unless you're honest."

Kelsey sighed. She knew her sister was right. She knew this was the reason she'd been unable to sleep. But why couldn't she have some time with Tyler before she told him the truth and hurt him again. Why couldn't they at least get through the wedding and Christmas? Then she would be honest with him. Then she would hurt him again and risk the relationship. Though she didn't want it to end.

"I know it's probably wrong, but right now it feels right."

She hated the military because it kept her from him, but it was his life and she loved Tyler, so she had to either accept he was a Marine and learn to live with his deployments or end it with him.

Right now was such a honeymoon phase for the two of them, but could she accept living without him when he was deployed once again? Could she learn to live with the lonely nights, the worrying, the fear and never hearing from him? She hadn't been able to do it before. Could she do it now?

"You're right. I should tell him the truth, but I'm not going to do anything until after your wedding and Christmas. Maybe it's selfish, but I want this time with him."

Her sister shook her head, her facial expression screaming Kelsey was making a huge mistake, but she wanted this time with Tyler for as long as possible.

"Then you better hope and pray he doesn't get his memory back."

Kelsey squeezed her eyes shut. She was taking a huge chance. She was risking so much, but it was all because she'd made a mistake she was trying to rectify. Maybe he would never remember and maybe she should be honest with him, but maybe she just wanted things to continue the way they were going.

Deliriously happy, why couldn't things stay the way they were and he'd never be deployed again and they could live their lives the way they were at this moment? That would be her dream solution.

Right now she wasn't willing to give him up for any reason, not the truth or the military. He was hers for this time and she wasn't going to let anything mar their time together.

~

Tyler kept waiting for Kelsey to return with her sister in tow. The two of them were close and he was sure they were holed up somewhere while Kelsey told her the truth about why he was home. He glanced around the room at his old friends, acquaintances from college and high school friends he'd known for twenty years and felt disconnected.

"Hey, Tyler," a young woman said walking by. "Great to see you're home."

"Thanks," he said, turning away.

It seemed strange to be here enjoying this celebration, while his troops were back in the desert still fighting the enemy, still trying to find the insurgents and rescue the innocent and stay alive.

All while he was at a wedding shower, where the bride and groom would be inundated with gifts. Life here in the States now seemed rather frivolous compared to what he'd witnessed in the desert. Family was just as important there as it was here. There was still a hierarchy of wealth and privilege in each village. Women had little or no respect and girls were married at such a young age that it sickened him.

"You doing okay," Jared asked him as he walked by his hands full of gifts.

"Doing great," Tyler lied, wanting Kelsey and wishing they could leave. He felt out of place.

Sure, he felt blessed to live here. But so much seemed trivial compared to what he'd dealt with while being deployed. And while he was in no hurry to return to war, he knew without a doubt that he'd come home a different man. A much more serious man than the fun-loving boy who'd gone to war.

"Who's going to the Super Bowl?" a man asked.

The discussion was off and going about which team deserved to go to the finals.

Watching his friends talking about which team was going to make it to the playoffs seemed so mundane and ordinary. These people had no clue what it was like to see a village destroyed by the enemy. To see children being used as targets. Some days the task had seemed like they were mice fighting Godzilla and other days he'd gone to sleep feeling like Mother Teresa.

Funny how four years of military training hadn't prepared him for the reality of the situation. Even without his memory, he remembered enough to know it'd been nothing like he expected.

It was odd he couldn't remember how he'd fallen fighting the war, but remember the everyday mundane stuff. But then again, he felt odd being here in this room, watching his friends and feeling like he was on the outside gazing in.

"Hey, man, glad to see you're alive and kicking," Joe, a friend from college, walked over and patted him on the back.

"Thanks, good to see you too."

Tyler gave a quick glance at his watch, wondering how much longer this party would go on.

"I was kind of shocked to see you and Kelsey walk in the door. I heard the two of you were done," he said.

"What?" he said shock gripping him as he shook his head. "No man, we're tighter than ever," he said, rubbing his head as an ache seemed to penetrate his skull. Why had he ever thought that parties were fun? This one had just begun and already he was ready to leave. To escape and take Kelsey back to the house and ravish her sweet body.

"What made you think we broke up?" Tyler asked.

"Oh, I just heard a rumor. Obviously it was wrong."

"Obviously. Strange how rumors get started," Tyler rubbed his head as an ache begin in earnest. Maybe he could persuade Kelsey to leave early.

"Great. Glad I didn't ask her out," Joe said with a laugh. "I considered it."

Jealousy zinged through Tyler, but he shrugged it off, knowing that Kelsey thought Joe was a lazy, lame excuse for a man. "Not to worry, she would have said no."

"Great to see you," Joe said, shaking his head and walking off.

He'd never liked the guy and now that he knew he'd been eyeing his girl, the distaste rose like bile in his throat. When would this party end?

Jared brought him a Coke to drink. "What did that ass-hat want?"

"Said he thought about asking Kelsey out because he thought we'd broken up."

Jared gazed at him strangely. "Dickhead."

"No worries. Kelsey would never have gone," Tyler said with conviction. He knew his girl and he had no worries about her cheating on him. She didn't like the military, but he hoped eventually she would come to accept that this was his life.

As a child, he'd watched his mom deal with his father's deployments. After a while the whole family had just known there were months Dad was gone. But when he came home they all celebrated and made adjustments to him coming back into their lives.

Jared shifted uneasily just as Kelsey and Sara walked into the kitchen. "Here come the girls."

"Man, we're blessed to be dating the hottest sisters in town," Tyler said with a laugh.

How had he gotten so lucky? Kelsey was beautiful and smart and he couldn't wait for them to begin their life together.

"Yeah," Jared said. "I hope in twenty years, we still feel that way."

"Of course we will," Tyler said, watching as Kelsey walked across the room, eager to get home and peel that clingy sweater dress from her rounded curves. She smiled at him and he felt it all the way to his toes as his heart warmed and he hardened just gazing at her. They had been dating for two years and he'd asked her to marry him right before he'd left for Afghanistan.

"You're lucky, man," Tyler said. "You'll be married soon."

Seeing Kelsey last night had made him realize just how fortunate he was to have her. What other girlfriend would have gotten up with him, when his leg was aching, given him an ice pack, insisted on him taking one of his muscle relaxers and urged him back to bed. He'd been surprised when he'd fallen back asleep and could only contribute it to being with Kelsey. In the hospital, he'd lain awake for hours fighting the pain, fearing the unknown and trying to remember.

"Kind of scary," Jared said. "With the divorce rate, you just never know."

"You two will be fine," Tyler assured. "Just like me and Kelsey."

Jared frowned, but didn't respond and Tyler chalked it up to wedding nerves.

Tyler tried to stay focused on his friend, but memories of the night before kept flashing into his brain. How Kelsey had wrapped her arms around him, holding him until he'd fallen asleep. He soon felt himself relax and had the best night of sleep he'd had in months. This morning he awakened feeling refreshed, surrounded by her womanly curves and hard as a rocket. He sighed at the image of how they'd spent the morning.

"Looks like it's time to open presents," Jared said.

"Better get started," Tyler said, sighing with relief. Maybe they could leave soon.

"You okay?" Kelsey asked walking up to him, her big green eyes questioning.

"I'm fine," he replied, remembering how many times she'd come apart in his arms this morning. Somehow he'd been afraid his dick wouldn't perform correctly after all the poking and probing the doctors had done to him in the hospital, but so far, it was functioning perfectly and he intended to use it all he could while he was home.

He grinned at her, leaned down close to her ear. "How long do we have to stay?"

She giggled and glanced up at him. "At least until they've opened all the wedding presents."

"Tyler," called a friend.

He whirled around at the voice, cringing inside. He really wasn't in the mood for more getting reacquainted. "Mike. How are you, man?"

"Kelsey, hello," he said, staring between the two of them. "Good to see you two together."

"Thanks, Mike," Kelsey said, smiling.

"You know when I'm home, I'm with Kelsey," Tyler said, confused by the man's remarks. Some of their friends seemed to be under the impression they were no longer together and that shocked him. Why in the world would they think that?

"Great, you home long?"

"Just until I recover enough, they think I'm ready to return to duty," Tyler said, knowing that while part of him dreaded going back, the marine in him was eager to return to his outfit. He loved the regiment of the Marines, of knowing what was expected of him and what his goals and objectives were and how you were trained to reach that mark, no matter what the cost. Even if it meant your life.

"Let's grab lunch before you head back," Mike said.

"Sure, but it has to be after the holidays. We've got this wedding and then Christmas."

Right now he wanted to focus on Kelsey. Those weeks she was out of school, would be their time. He couldn't wait for this wedding to be over and for them to spend the holidays together.

"Give me a call," he said, and walked off.

Glancing down at Kelsey, he noticed how white she was. "You okay?"

"Just felt a little nauseous there for a moment. We didn't eat breakfast and while I've had some great snacks here, I think I'm needing a decent meal."

He was so ready to leave. While he knew everyone here didn't understand, he just wasn't in a partying kind of mood. He was still healing and maybe that bomb had done something to his psyche because he didn't like being in crowds any longer. He just wanted to stay home with Kelsey by his side.

"Yeah, let's go out and celebrate as soon as this is over. You can take me to a really nice restaurant, wine and dine and then sixty-nine me," he whispered against her ear, wishing they could leave right now.

The thought of being alone with her was enough to have him looking for his coat.

She hit him on the arm. "Pervert."

He hugged her close. "You bet I am. Can't you get your sister to open those presents any faster?"

She giggled. "Settle down big boy. It's going to be a while."

~

Kelsey couldn't wait to leave the wedding shower any longer. She couldn't believe that Mike said something about the two of them being together. Thank goodness that Tyler didn't seem to make the connection that Mike believed them to have broken up.

She was certain he was going to learn the truth right there at the party, at that moment. She'd wanted to grab his hand and run to the nearest exit. It had almost been a choice of do I stay for my sister and risk losing my love, or do I leave right now in order to protect my relationship with Tyler.

She'd felt so conflicted and he'd realized that something was wrong when he asked her if she was feeling okay. What could she say? *Oh, I just about had a heart attack when Mike told you we'd broken up?*

She released a deep sigh and he glanced over at her. "That was some wedding shower."

"Yeah, I think it's great how it's no longer just a girl event. I like it when the groom and his buddies are invited as well."

While she had looked forward to the event for weeks, it had been way too stressful for her to enjoy. Even the glass of wine her sister had given her, hadn't released the tension in her body.

"Your sister even let Jared open some presents."

"She likes to share."

For a moment she watched as Tyler drove her car through the traffic. At first she'd been afraid to let him drive. His leg was injured, but it was his left leg, so she'd decided it would be good for him.

The bandage was still wrapped around his head, but they were going to remove it before the wedding. The doctors had told him he could take it off five days after arriving and that would be right before the wedding and all the pictures. Of course, the cut would still show, but Sara and Jared had assured him they didn't care. They wanted him in their wedding.

"So when we get married are you going to want a big to-do like what Sara and Jared are having?"

Her heart gave a little lurch at the idea of them saying I do. Right now, she wanted that more than anything, but how would she feel when he left again? Could she take him constantly being in danger? Of being gone? What if he died?

"I don't think so. This has been a lot of work. I'd be happy just you and me and the people we love and a minister."

It was true. While her sister's wedding would be lovely, Kelsey wanted something a little more intimate.

He glanced over at her. "Wow, I'm shocked to hear that."

"Why?"

"I just expected you to want a big church wedding."

If Kelsey had her way, her and Tyler would elope. If guilt didn't plague her and she felt more confident in herself as a military wife, she'd suggest they get married tonight, right this moment. But she knew that wouldn't be right.

"It took Sara and Jared over a year to plan this event. It cost my parents a small fortune and while I will want wedding photos, I just think I'd like it to be small. More private and intimate."

Silence filled the car as they drove toward the restaurant. It was comfortable, just the two of them and she glanced at Tyler, wishing he didn't have to leave.

"You know you never told me how you managed while I was gone?" he asked.

Had all the questions regarding whether or not they were together, suddenly made him suspicious? She'd failed miserably at being a marine's girlfriend, but she wasn't ready to tell him that just yet. Somehow they had to get through the wedding and Christmas and then she would decide how much she thought he should know about her implosion.

"What do you mean?" she asked, her head turning to gaze at him as car lights flashed into the car. This was a conversation she didn't want to have. How could she confess that she'd sucked at being a military girlfriend.

"Since I can't remember your letters, I was curious as to how you handled being alone? How did you deal with it? Did you get involved with the other military wives? You need a marine sister to help you cope when I'm gone."

What could she say? She'd gone into her home and hibernated, only coming out for work and when she'd been dragged away from the television, searching the news channels for any news related to the military.

She swallowed. "I missed you terribly. I was lonely. My sister and friends tried to keep me busy and not let me think of all the danger you were in. But I have to say at night, it was hard. I was scared. And not hearing from you was the worst."

With his injuries how could she tell him that she'd worried nonstop about him getting hurt. She'd cried herself to sleep at night and had become a news junkie searching for anything about what was going on in Afghanistan. Terrified when she heard that soldiers had been killed or kidnapped.

He reached out and patted her on the leg. "I can't promise it will ever get any easier."

"I know."

Why did she feel like she was walking along a high bridge covered in ice. One wrong move and she'd go plunging over the side.

"It was good to see our friends from college. Except that dickhead Joe. He said something really weird to me."

Her heart leaped into her throat at the mention of Joe's name and she felt the urge to use duct tape on that man's mouth. That guy was a moron and if anyone would say something really stupid that would make Tyler wonder, it would be him. Why had she thought they could attend her sister's wedding shower together? Why?

"What did he say?" she asked, trying to sound surprised.

"He said he thought it was weird seeing us together again?"

"What?" she said, giving an academy award performance. "Why would he say that?"

Tyler was silent for a moment as he drove through traffic. Finally, the cars thinned out. "Said he thought about asking you on a date."

"He should donate his brain to science. Maybe they could find a cure."

Tyler laughed.

"Really, he told you he was going to ask me out on a date? He'd have a better chance of getting a snowball into hell."

Tyler squeezed her leg. "I know, honey. I thought you would get a kick out of it. But it was weird that there was a rumor going around about the two of us breaking up."

"People are just jealous of what we have. They'd love to see us split up, because they can't find this kind of happiness."

Somehow it felt like she'd been in a mine field and she'd been dodging land mines. One wrong step and everything would blow up.

He turned and glanced at her. "You're right. We're happy."

"I love you to the moon and back, Tyler Ferguson."

"I'm glad."

Silence filled the car and Kelsey felt her heart hammering in her chest. She didn't want to tell him the truth, but if she didn't some ass-hat was going to let him know of her weakness and convince him of the truth.

And this time she didn't know if he would forgive her for not only abandoning him, but lying to him as well. Her sister was right and yet she just didn't have the strength or the desire to talk about it now. Not yet, when everything was perfect.

They pulled into the restaurant parking lot where there were few cars. Getting out, Tyler came around and opened her door. Helping her out, she smiled up at him. "Thank you."

Holding hands they walked into the restaurant and were promptly seated. As they gazed over the menu, she glanced around. "Remember when you brought me here the last time? It was right before you were deployed. You were flying out the next morning and we ate dinner, then made love all night long."

That night had been hell. She'd cherished every moment over the next few months, hoping it wouldn't be their last time together.

He laughed. "Oh yeah, I remember that very well. I slept all the way to Afghanistan. And when I arrived, it was one hundred and ten."

"Why is it you can remember some things, but not others? I would never have thought you would remember landing in Afghanistan."

She feared that at any moment, he was going to tell her, his memory had returned.

Gazing at her, he shook his head. "It's like there is a black hole from almost that day until I woke up in the hospital. I remember my men, their names, their faces. Even what we had for breakfast that first day, but after that nothing."

Inside, her heart was breaking for him. Her sister was right, there was a giant part of him missing and yet she wasn't ready for his memory to return.

"So tell me about your class," Tyler said changing the subject.

Kelsey realized he was tired of the focus being on his problems. She smiled, she loved her job, she loved the age that she taught. They were still such innocents and eager to learn, untarnished by the world. Besides the occasional disciplinary problem, the only thing she didn't like about her job was the parents. Sometimes they were harder to deal with than the children.

"This year my class is probably the best one I've had to date. There are probably two kids in there that if they're not a genius, they have near genius IQ. I have one budding rock star and two girls that if they aren't the next generation of celebrity housewives, I'd be shocked. They're so fun to watch and see them changing every day right before my eyes."

She really did enjoy teaching and her children were precious gifts she got to instruct and help on their education path.

"But they're so young," he said.

"That's why they're so much fun. Most of them are eager to learn. They are each vying for attention, trying to outdo the other one. And the girls are already trying to get boys attention, and the boys, they just want to appear tough. It's so interesting watching the dynamics."

Tyler shook his head. "I think you're the only person I know who enjoys being around twenty five-year-olds."

He reached out and grasped her hand, leaned forward and stared into her eyes. The sound of a champagne bottle popping resounded and Kelsey watched his eyes grow wide, they clouded over and his face tightened. His grip squeezed her hand almost hurting her.

"Incoming," he screamed yanking her beneath the table. "Stay down."

"Tyler," she said, her voice choking. "Tyler, it's okay."

He didn't see her, he didn't respond as he gazed out from under the tablecloth looking around. She realized he wasn't here, he was back in Afghanistan trying to stay alive. She touched his arm, rubbing it with her hand. "Baby, come back to me. We're safe. We're okay. We're here in Denver."

Suddenly his body sagged and he started to shake. It had lasted less than five minutes, but she could see the turmoil in his eyes, the fear etched on his face.

"Oh God, Kelsey. I'm sorry."

She pulled him into her arms, beneath the table. "It's okay."

"I... I don't know what happened, but suddenly I was back there. Hell," he said with a sigh.

She rubbed his back. "My sweet man. You're here with me."

Sweat soaked through his shirt and she could feel his body trembling and still she held him beneath the table, with the linen cloth covering them, the clink of dishes continuing in the restaurant.

"Do you mind if we skip dinner and go home?" he asked.

"Let's go," she said. "We can have pizza delivered and watch a movie in our pajamas."

"God, I don't deserve you," he whispered against her neck and her heart clenched with pain. If he ever learned the truth, he'd hate her and yet how could she top more misery on him. She couldn't and she wouldn't, she didn't care what Sara thought. She could not tell Tyler the truth. At least not right now.

"Let's go home," she said, giving him a squeeze as she crawled out from under the table. When she came out the waiter was standing there, staring.

"Is everything okay?" he asked.

"Sorry, I lost an earring," she said with a smile.

The waiter gave her a puzzled look and she could see he didn't believe her, but frankly she didn't care. Tyler stood and glanced around like he was making sure that the sound he'd heard was just the champagne bottle.

"I think we're going to skip dinner tonight, we've decided we have dessert waiting for us at home. Could you please get us our check," she said. Let the waiter think what he wanted. She needed to get her man home and let him relax.

Tyler's injuries were more than skin deep. Slowly, she was learning the extent of what that bomb had done to him and while she was so thankful he'd lived through the experience, the thought of sending him back was more than she could bear after seeing him cowering under that table.

The waiter brought the check and she grabbed it. Tyler was still obviously shaken as he stared off into space, like he wasn't with her one hundred percent. She just wanted to get him home where she could help him.

As they walked out the door, she glanced at him and noticed the pallor of his skin was even whiter than earlier. Sweat beaded his upper lip and his hands trembled.

"Are you all right?" she asked as she stared at him worriedly. Without asking she climbed behind the wheel of the car as he sank into the seat beside her.

He reached up and rubbed his head in a way that she was quickly learning meant he had a headache. "Do you have any aspirin in your purse."

"Yes," she said, grabbing it and pulling out a small bottle. She handed him two and watched as he quickly swallowed them without water. "What's wrong? Should I take you to the hospital."

He shook his head. "No." He placed his head in his hands and started shaking again.

"Tell me what's wrong?"

"I remembered the explosion. The force of the blast as it slung me from the vehicle out into the sand. I remember lying there thinking I was going to die."

Chapter Four

The next morning, while Tyler was in the shower, she pulled out her laptop and quickly started doing a search for brain injuries, amnesia and finally PTSD. Her engagement ring sparkled on her left hand. Everything she read made her realize how lucky Tyler was to have only lost his memory.

The facts about traumatic brain injuries of people having to relearn the simplest tasks frightened her. Some people had to learn to walk, talk and even how to read all over again and she said a quick prayer thanking God he'd survived with just the bodily damage he had and another one for anyone suffering the horrible things she'd read about.

How did soldiers' families deal with not only their physical wounds but also post-traumatic stress episodes. The littlest thing could send him running for cover and she suddenly worried about the meeting she'd scheduled with her class.

She would never want to expose these children she cared so much about to Tyler freaking out. And Tyler would be humiliated if he scared the children. She still wanted him to come, but she would do everything she could to make certain that nothing happened.

She picked up the phone and called her sister, unable to wait another minute even though it was only six thirty in the morning. But she had to talk to someone.

The phone rang and finally her sister answered, her sleepy voice dazed. "Someone better be either dead or bleeding for you to call me this early in the morning."

Kelsey laughed. "Everyone is fine, but I had to talk. I'm scared."

"With good reason," her sister said groggily. She paused and Kelsey could almost see her face frowning over the phone as she woke up enough to realize there was a problem. "What's wrong? Is Tyler okay?"

"Tyler had an episode of PTSD last night."

"What happened," she said, her voice suddenly rising in intensity.

Kelsey quickly told her sister about them crawling under the table at one of the finest restaurants in town. She wasn't ashamed, she'd been scared. And now when she knew the truth about what could happen when he had one of these episodes, she was even more frightened.

"But the worst thing is that he remembered the explosion."

That sounded so awful. Those words spilling from her lips was enough to make her want to choke. She should be happy he was beginning to recall events. But it terrified her.

The phone went silent for a moment. Then her sister said the words she didn't want to hear, the words she was most afraid of.

"You know this could mean his memory is returning."

"No, not yet." She didn't want him to recall his past. She wanted things to continue just like they were.

"Kelsey, you have no control over when his memory is going to return. Please tell him the truth."

"After your wedding and Christmas. I just want to spend Christmas with him, then I'll confess, but we're so happy."

Even with his injuries, things were great between them right now. The military wasn't trying to take him away from her. The prospect of him being stationed here in the States was looking better and better, the longer his memory didn't return. Selfishly, she wanted him here sitting in a safe office.

Before he left for Afghanistan, they'd been fighting about his commitment to the military. She hadn't wanted him to leave and he'd been insistent that this was his duty, his calling.

Maybe she was self-centered, but she just wanted him home with her. Safe and sound and let someone else put their life on the line to protect that piece of desert that meant nothing to her.

"Oh, Kelsey, you're setting yourself up for heartache."

"Is it wrong to hope that he won't remember?"

"Yes. How would you like to have a bit of time missing from your memory? I can't imagine not knowing what happened. You wouldn't know what had changed you. Do you understand."

Kelsey sighed. Of course she would hate not knowing. She was being selfish, she knew it, but it was only because she didn't want to hurt him. Hasn't he experienced enough pain at her hands? She only wanted to protect him from the hurt she'd created.

"I do. I just don't want him to suffer anymore. He's been through enough."

Suddenly the bathroom door opened and he stood there, a towel wrapped around his waist, his hair gleaming wet, his muscled abs so well defined, that she had to swallow to keep the desire from drowning her.

"Thanks for letting me know about the wedding changes. I've got to run. It's my turn to grab a shower."

A cold one if she was lucky.

"Oh, he's come out and you're no longer alone. I understand. If you want to talk some more, call me later. But Kelsey, tell him the truth and do it before his memory returns."

"Thanks, Sara, talk to you later. Love you," she said.

"Next time you call me at this hour, it better not be while I'm on my honeymoon."

Kelsey giggled. "Goodbye."

"Love you," she said and hung up the phone.

In so many ways, Kelsey felt blessed. She had a loving family, her sister was her best friend and she'd been given a great education and the opportunity to have a good life. Hopefully, she hadn't screwed up her chance for a loving life with Tyler.

She glanced over at her man and he dropped the towel. She swallowed, her blood rushing through her at the sight of her beautiful soldier.

He grinned at her. "I thought that maybe we would work up an appetite for breakfast."

How could she resist.

~

Friday afternoon, the last day of school before Christmas break, the kids were running on pure adrenaline. Eager for the party, the last hour before they began their Christmas vacation, anxious that Santa Claus would remember to stop at their house and deliver the toys they'd requested.

In her class, she was fortunate that every one of her children came from families who seemed to at least give off the air of affluence. As a class project, they had each brought a new toy to give to a less fortunate child. She was trying to instill in her students a benefactor spirit. Today, not only was Tyler coming to her class, but he was going to take the toys her kids had collected for Toys for Tots. Her big strong marine would arrive in his dress clothes, surprise the children and pick up their donation.

"Miss Johnson how much longer?"

Later, after her class had gone out the door, she would meet up with Tyler and they would go Christmas tree shopping. He'd already been questioning why she hadn't hung up her normal decorations, but she seemed lacking in Christmas spirit this year and she'd been busy missing Tyler, helping her sister prepare for the wedding.

"James what time does the clock on the wall show?"

How could she explain to him that she'd been heart sick after ending their relationship and putting Santa and the reindeer on her front lawn just hadn't appealed to her. Usually her yard looked like someone vomited Christmas lights on her front lawn, tossing in Santa and some angels amongst the bulbs. But not this year.

Trying to keep her mind on the job at hand, she noticed that her complaining student was acting surly.

He'd slumped down in his desk and crossed his arms, a pouting expression on his face. "One one five."

"No, that's not right. Try again," she said.

"One fifteen."

"Perfect. What time did I tell you the party started?"

"Two o'clock. How long do you have to wait?"

She watched him counting up the minutes on his fingers and smiled. Today, she'd let him get away with his addition.

"Forty-five minutes."

"Good job."

The boy smiled, his dimples creasing his cheeks.

"So let's go over your holiday homework."

There was a unanimous groan. "I've given you two papers to complete and bring back. One is on numbers and one is the alphabet. Anyone who reads a book and comes back to tell me about it, gets a chance to draw from the goodie bag."

She kept a bag filled with small prizes for those students who really tried or went a step above and beyond on their classwork. Usually she didn't announce it in advance, but she wanted to give her class some incentive to read while they were on Christmas vacation.

"Everyone clean off their desks. We're going to read a story until party time."

There was a quick shuffling of papers, being shoved into their backpacks, desks being cleared. Her students looked eagerly toward her.

When the noise settled and the children were staring at her, she began to read <u>The Night Before Christmas</u>.

While she was reading, several of the room moms arrived and began to set up the Christmas party, where each child would receive a gift bag and be served cookies and punch. The children were growing restless, but she continued on waiting for her soldier to arrive.

Finally, the door sprang open and in walked Tyler in his full dress uniform, looking more handsome than a man had a right to. The children gasped in awe at the sight of Tyler.

A rush of pride filled Kelsey. Her big, strong, uniformed man strode into the room wearing his dress blues, walked right down in front of her, in his military stance and clicked his heels together. "Second Lieutenant Tyler Ferguson of the U.S. Marines, to pick up the toys your class generously donated."

She smiled at him. "Boys and girls, this is my fiancé and as a Christmas surprise, he's going to tell you a little bit about the Marine Corp."

The boys stared at him in awe and the girls gazed at him, their eyes wide.

"Good afternoon," he said in his military voice. "The Marine Corp began in 1775 during the revolutionary war."

While Kelsey listened to him tell the children about the marines, she couldn't help but notice his enthusiasm for what he did. What if she could no longer teach? How would that make her feel?

He paused for a moment and gazed at the students. "Do you have any questions?"

Several hands shot up reaching for the sky.

"Have you ever been shot at?" one kid asked.

"Yes," he said not going into details for which she was glad. These children didn't need to hear the gory details of war. She'd seen more of the effect of war on men than she wanted by being his fiancé.

"Have you ever been hurt?"

"Yes," he replied. "I took a piece of shrapnel in the leg."

"What's shrapnel?" another kid asked.

"It's a piece of metal."

"Ouch," the boy said.

Kelsey was so proud of how he was responding. He was answering their questions, but not giving them too much information. They were still innocents and she didn't want them to know too much, just introduce them to a soldier.

"Do you miss your friends and family when you go away," a little girl asked.

"Very much," he responded. "I'm usually gone a long time."

"Do you use your sword to kill bad men?"

He smiled at the young boy. "We no longer wear swords in battle. But if I needed to use it, the blade is sharp enough to hurt someone."

"Cool," the child said. "Like a pirate."

One of the boys, her rowdiest kid in class, knocked over a chair trying to get Tyler's attention. The chair crashed to the floor and Kelsey tensed watching Tyler, fearing the worst. That horrible glaze appeared in his eyes and she watched him, panic spiraling through her. His hand went to where his gun should be. Just then a little girl giggled.

Tyler shook his head, released a big sigh and relief rushed through Kelsey. He'd gone to that terrible place, but he was back.

He gave the boy a tense smile and she could see the effort it took him.

"You okay, son?" he asked.

"Yes."

Things were back to normal. Maybe this hadn't been such a good idea. It could have been so much worse. Her man was still injured and in need of her protection.

"What's your question?"

"Have you ever shot and killed anyone?"

"My job as a soldier, is to protect our country. The only time I fire my weapon is when I'm defending our freedoms. So yes, I have fired my weapon."

That last question, was enough to make her decide it was time to end his visit. The children had learned enough. She didn't want her students going home and telling their parents a marine came to class and told them how he killed people or had he thought he was back in the war.

"I think the mothers are ready for us, and it's time we had our Christmas party."

"Yeah," they all yelled, their attention diverted.

"Everyone line up."

As the room mother's handed out cookies and punch, another mother laid gift bags on the desks.

"They're a great bunch of kids," Tyler said, walking up to her and touching her arm. Warmth rushed through her at the feel of his hand, making her smile. Only Tyler had ever created such a reaction.

"Thanks for coming and talking to them."

"My pleasure," he said with a smile that had tingles going from her toes to her head and back up again. To think, she'd given up this amazing man had her doubting herself. Just gazing at him made her think she needed to be committed. What had she been thinking?

James, her rambunctious student ran up. "You and Miss Johnson are going to get married?"

"Eventually," Tyler said to the young man.

"Ewww...are you going to kiss her."

"James, that's not a question you ask," Kelsey told the boy.

"Kiss her, kiss her, kiss her," the kids started chanting.

She shook her head at Tyler knowing the school would not think it was appropriate behavior for a teacher to kiss in front of her students.

Tyler, picked up her hand, bent over and elegantly kissed the back of it, letting his tongue linger, sending shivers through her, while the room mothers smiled. It was the perfect solution and she grinned at her big soldier man.

"I better go," he said.

Walking over to the toys, he shook out a big red sack and quickly loaded their gifts into the bag. He turned back to the children. "The United States Marine Corp and Toys for Tots thank you for your donation. Merry Christmas, everyone."

Part of her couldn't help but worry about him driving through town alone. What if he had another episode. What if he freaked out and she wasn't there? But she had to let him go. She couldn't hold him back.

The kids started jumping up and down and calling out Merry Christmas as Tyler walked out the door. At the last second he turned back to her and winked.

Her heart overflowed with love and tears filled her eyes. How could she live without him? But how could she watch him go off to war again, knowing this time he might come back in even worse shape or not at all.

Chapter Five

Tyler and Kelsey lugged the tree into the house, with her carrying the top and him the trunk. Exhaustion ached from every bone, a reminder of how he was still not completely healed from the explosion he could now remember.

At the thought he realized how he hadn't heard anything while he'd lay in the sand, pain rocketing through his body, thinking he was going to die. Of all the memories he wanted to return, this was not the one he desired the most.

Snapping back to the present, he heard her call out, "Easy, one of the branches is hung on the frame of the door."

He'd been on his feet for longer than he should and his leg was beginning to ache. They'd had the tree farm cut the end off and shape up the tree, so all he had to do was drop the trunk into the stand and then he could rest and watch her decorate.

She carried her part of the tree into the living room of the cozy house. "I don't think we should put it next to the fireplace."

"No, too big a fire hazard."

"And I don't want it too far from the window. I want my neighbors to see the lights, all lit up."

"Okay, where do you want it to stand?"

All he could think about was sitting down, not where to put this damn tree. But it was important to her and he refused to let her see his weakness. His damn leg was healing at a much faster rate than his mind and yet both were slower than he preferred. How could one tiny piece of metal cause so much pain in his leg? And how could his mind still refuse to return to normal?

Today when one of her kids knocked over the chair, sending his mind back into combat mode he'd struggled to overcome the urge to issue commands, warning everyone to take cover. Thank God, he'd managed to push back the demons of war in the presence of those children.

He wouldn't be standing in front of a classroom again for a long time. There was no need to risk exposing children to his nightmares.

Kelsey glanced around the room and he wanted to say, hurry, but didn't. "What if we put it in the corner?"

"Perfect," he said not really caring.

She grabbed the stand and he dropped the trunk into the holder. Several minutes later, after they were finished making certain it was straight, she took his hand and led him to the couch. "Come on, let's sit for a minute and catch our breath."

Wearily he sank onto the couch. It felt good to get off his leg. Memories of his parents decorating for Christmas filled him. His father would grouch about the tree, but everyone knew it was fake. As soon as he set up the stand, then Tyler, his brothers, and his mother would string the lights and hang the bulbs, while his father sat back and watched.

His dad never participated in the decorating, but the next day he would drag out the yard decorations and make certain that Santa Claus was waving to the street and the reindeer were visible.

Tyler had great Christmas memories with his family and he missed them. Today his mother lived near his older brother in Chicago in an Alzheimer's care unit. Maybe he and Kelsey would have time during the holidays to visit them. He needed to spend some time with his family while he was on leave. But frankly, all he could think about was Kelsey and that's why he'd come home to Denver.

When he'd left for Afghanistan, he and Kelsey had been fighting. Not over how much they loved each other, because of her insistence for him to give up the Marines and take a nine-to-five job. Even the idea, sounded boring.

He was living his dream, doing what he was called to become and she had to accept he would never be a desk jockey until gray appeared in his hair.

"What was your favorite Christmas present you received as a child," she asked him staring at their tree.

"Easy. A bicycle so I could ride with my older brothers. What about you?"

Their conversation tugged at his chest, leaving an ache, bringing back even more memories of his family Christmas, making him wish he could visit at least with his brothers.

"A Barbie playhouse and Sara got the Barbie car. We had more doll stuff than any of the girls on our block."

He ran his hand through his hair, wanting to change the direction of his thoughts. "What kind of toys do you think our kids will want?"

She grinned at him. "Video games, bicycles, whatever their friends are getting for Christmas."

"I guess, the first question I should have asked was if you wanted kids," he said, knowing instinctively she did. Or at least hoping his assumptions were correct.

"I'd like to have a couple. Two, maybe three," she said. "What about you? Do you want a couple of rug rats?"

Wrapping his arm around her, he gazed into her green eyes, unable to keep from staring. Her eyes reminded him of a forest he wanted to wander in forever. "I want as many kids with you as we can have. I'd like a whole team of rug rats. Especially if they look like you."

She snuggled up against him and he leaned in and kissed her on the lips. Frankly, he'd like nothing better for them to start practicing, trying to have those babies right now. He was up for the challenge.

Placing her hand on his chest, she leaned back. "Is it okay if we wait a few years after we're married before we start working on this team. I'd like to have some time alone with you before we begin our family that we'll have the rest of our lives."

He hugged her close. "I think spending time just the two of us, buying a house and getting our lives in order is a great idea."

Knowing that so many months of the year, he'd be gone, opened a cavern of pain in his heart. When she said yes, they would probably only get to see each other two - three months of each of those years. But whatever time they had together would be precious. And coming home to her and the children would be something to look forward to.

Jumping up, she pulled him to his feet. "If you help me decorate the tree, I'll let you kiss me under the mistletoe."

"You couldn't stop me from kissing you," he said, really wanting to keep as much pressure off his leg as possible, but knowing Kelsey enjoyed them working together to decorate the house for Christmas.

An ache began to radiate from his knee downward, but he refused to acknowledge the feeling.

She pulled the lights out of the box marked Christmas and began to weave them through the tree. He pulled out another string and began to wind them through the pine needles in the opposite direction.

The aroma of pine and Kelsey filled him, making him hard with wanting her.

"When you say you want as many kids as you can have, just how many is that number?" she asked connecting his lights to hers.

"I'd like at least four, maybe five," he said. "Of course, it would probably mean we'd have to use base housing."

"That many? Really? Do you not believe in birth control?"

Laughter bubbled up from his chest. "I was lucky. I had a great childhood as a military brat and I guess I want to make certain I have a whole herd of kids who get the same experience."

Shaking her head with a smile she asked, "At what base?"

He shrugged. "Wherever I'm stationed. We might even go overseas for a while. I'd love to be deployed out of Germany and have you close by."

With her overseas, they could get to see each other more often. If they had children, it would be easier. She could possibly teach at the base school.

"I was five when dad was stationed in Germany. We spent his free time exploring Europe. We even skied in Switzerland."

"You were lucky," she said connecting another set of lights.

It was quiet for a few minutes before she asked, "Where did your family spend Christmas?"

The question brought back the memories he'd tried to push away. Being the youngest, life had certainly changed for his family. He remembered the fun times they had when he was a small boy, living in military housing in a foreign country.

"Every two years we were stationed in a different city. We spent Christmas in Okinawa, Japan, Stuttgart, Germany and even the United Kingdom. Plus we lived all over the United States."

They had friends, but his brothers were the ones who stuck close to him. It was a wonder he'd lived to see his tenth birthday with his older brothers practicing being Evel Knievel stunts on their bicycles as they jumped over his body. Once his older brother Scott landed on his arm, breaking it in two places. His mother had punished them all for being so reckless. They'd spent Christmas Day at the military hospital instead of playing with their new toys.

And Christmas had always been filled with presents, stockings and his mother's cooking.

"What about your father?"

The old man had not lived long after he retired from the service. A heart attack had struck him at the young age of sixty, leaving his mother alone. Permanently.

"He was only home for six Christmases that I can remember before he retired. While I was in college, he was home."

She frowned. "He missed so much of your childhood."

"Yes and no," he said, knowing she was thinking about their children and how much he would be home. "He was always there for the most important things. But the normal day-to-day activities, he had to work. Probably, no different than a man who works a job where he travels all the time."

"I can't imagine what your mother must have gone through. Dealing with children by herself."

"She was definitely a strong-willed woman until Alzheimer's claimed her."

"Have you been to visit?"

The last time he saw his mother, she hadn't remembered his name, just his face and he'd left his brother's house crying, knowing instinctively she wouldn't remember him at all the next time he saw her. For that reason, he'd put off returning to his brother's. Instead, he'd come to see Kelsey.

"No, but I thought I'd try to see her before I go back." He started hanging the ornaments on the branches. He picked up a picture ornament. It was a young girl and he knew it was Kelsey. "You were a cute kid."

"Do you have any ornament pictures of you as a kid?"

"I don't know. I have pictures of me. Maybe we can get one made for you to hang on our family tree."

His older brother had all the family mementos packed away. He'd promised them all that they would get together when their mother was gone and go through their parents' things. And Tyler wasn't ready for that day.

She smiled at him. "That would be nice. Then we'll add pictures of our kids as they come along."

The thought of children with Kelsey soothed his battered spirit. Life with her seemed perfect, like it was meant to be and a calmness came over him. Though his memory had not completely returned, maybe he should marry her before he left. Not let another moment pass without her being his wife.

"I like that idea," he said, grinning at her as he hung two ornaments, hoping to get this done. "Tell me about your family Christmas."

Placing an ornament on the tree, she turned to him and laughed.

"My father always helped decorate the tree. It was considered a family night and Sara and I had to be home. My mother would have Christmas carols playing, snacks and all of us would hang the bulbs and garland. It was fun, except for the year that Sara got mad and hid all the decorations because she couldn't attend her boyfriend's party."

"Seems kind of extreme."

"Later, she learned he was also dating her friend."

"The joys of dating as a teenager."

"Yeah, she was careful until she met Jared."

For a moment he was silent as he hung the last of the ornaments wishing his father wasn't buried in the National Cemetery and his mother wasn't in an Alzheimer's care unit. It was tough watching someone slip away slowly, losing their memories.

His father was the lucky one; he wasn't there to watch his wife disappearing. What if it happened to him? Would Kelsey be there to change his diapers, feed him, and answer his same questions over and over?

She didn't want him to leave to go to Afghanistan. If she didn't support him when he was in the military, would she support him when he was old and senile? He didn't doubt that she loved him, only if that it was enough.

"I remember when I deported, you wanted this to be my last trip overseas. Do you still feel that way?"

Her forehead wrinkled as she drew her brow together. She thought for a moment, then sighed. "If I had my way, I would have you by my side, every night, every day. But I know you love what you do. It's your passion and I'm trying very hard to learn to accept your life. But it's difficult and there are times I falter. I realize in order to keep you in my life, I have to learn to be a Marine's wife."

The words washed over him like a soothing balm. At least she was trying. No, it wasn't perfect, but she hadn't walked away. He'd worried for so long that she would never be able to accept his way of life and now here she was reassuring him, letting him know she understood.

He came around the tree and kissed her solidly on the mouth. Not a passionate lip sucking, groping session, but more a thankful that finally he knew he could depend on her. When their mouths parted, he stared down into her eyes. "Thank you. I know that wasn't easy."

She kind of laughed and shook her head. "No. It wasn't. I went through hell to get this far. I'm still working on understanding because I know what it means to you. But I'm not perfect and I've made a lot of mistakes while you were gone."

He reached down into the box, glad to see they were almost done. "I'll do my best to make certain I consider your needs."

But how could he? He'd watched his mother struggle with his father being gone. His wife, would do the same. Didn't all married couples wrestle with some kind of issue?

What about Jared and Sara? Did they have something they were working through? Did they love each other enough to persevere the tough times? Marriage didn't look easy.

"Do you think Jared and Sara will be happy?" he asked, wondering about his best friend. They seemed like a great couple, but his friend had been a huge womanizer until he met Sara. He really liked Kelsey's sister and didn't want to see her hurt and hoped that his friend had changed.

"Sara is crazy about Jared. I worry, but he's never cheated, he's always been true to her, so I'm hoping he's finally settled down," she said wistfully.

"She's changed him," he said thoughtfully. "He's been open and honest with her. Just like you've been with me."

A frown creased her forehead and she glanced away.

"Don't make me sound so good. When you're gone, I get weak."

"How?" he asked fearful she had cheated on him. Just the thought of her being with another man while he was defending their country would crush him. Loyalty, endurance, dependability and unselfishness are just a few of the leadership traits of a good marine and what was expected from an officer's wife.

"I get afraid. I'm so scared something's going to happen to you. I start to doubt what we have. If it's worth waiting on you to come home or if I'll ever be a good enough wife. I'm not a good marine girlfriend."

Her words had his heart clenching painfully inside his chest. Placing the last ornament on the tree he turned to her, needing her honest answer. The one he feared more than anything.

"Did you cheat on me?"

She gasped. "No. I just got scared. I feared you would get injured or die. That you wouldn't come home different. And both things have been realized. You're not the same man who left here nine months ago. And you're injured."

"I get scared too," he said, realizing it was true. "You're back home living a normal life while I'm in the desert facing the enemy, watching people die or be injured. I know the war has changed me. But please don't give up on us." He walked around the tree and took her in his arms. "I fear you're going to decide this is not the life you want. You're going to dump me, and send me a Dear John letter. I can't tell you how many guys I've seen it happen too. They go away and their girlfriends find someone else."

"It's hard, Tyler," she whispered against his shirt. "I don't doubt my love for you. I doubt this life you've chosen and if I can live with it. In fact..."

He'd had enough. He couldn't listen to them expressing their fears a moment longer and needed to show her his emotions. Kelsey meant everything to him.

He leaned down and covered her lips with his. He ravaged her mouth, taking her lips prisoner, holding her against him, pouring his emotions into his kiss. The thought of her giving up on this life that he loved crushed his soul.

The military was ingrained in his blood, it was a part of his DNA. He'd known since high school that he would go into the military after college and here he was, first lieutenant. He'd worked hard to make it this far and realized every soldier in the United States had someone worried sick about them returning home.

She pushed back and gazed up into his eyes. "Put the star on the tree and take me to bed."

Releasing her, he grabbed the star out of the box and shoved it on top of the tree. "I thought you'd never ask."

She smiled up at him as he pulled her towards the bedroom.

~

Tyler quickly shed his clothes, wanting only to crawl into bed with this woman he loved. Their talk tonight left him nervous. Somehow he had to show her their relationship was worth the time he was gone.

He had to show her she was strong and he would always return home to her. She was his rock, his beacon in a world that was crazy and filled with death and destruction. She would always be there waiting for him, calling him home to spend time with her and someday their family.

This was what his mother had done for his father and what he longed for her to create for him. That oasis where his life would return to normal and he could put the pressures of battle behind him.

She slipped into bed beside him and he pulled her into his arms. "I need you, Kelsey. Don't ever doubt that I want you."

"I know Tyler. I need you as well. I'm so afraid that something will happen to you. What if you get killed? How will I live with you not being in my life? It's bad enough, you're not here every day, but to never see you again, I think I would die along with you."

"Don't ever forget that as a marine, courage is one of the leadership traits."

Her words did not make him feel better, in fact, they only showed the depth of her anxiety, her fear, and how could he promise her that nothing would happen to him, when he'd already been injured once.

"If I die, just know that the time I spent with you were the best years of my life. If I have my way, I'll die in your arms when I'm one hundred, not a minute before. But I could go tomorrow. So whatever time we have together is precious to me. And I take the memories with me when I leave you."

She clutched him, holding him tightly against her. "Oh Tyler. I don't deserve you."

"Just don't get scared and send me a Dear John letter. I don't think I could live with that."

She leaned back and placed her mouth over his. He could feel her body shaking and knew that she wanted him as much as he couldn't wait to get inside her. As her lips moved over his, kissing him like she'd never see him again, he truly thought how could life get any better than this? He was here with the woman he loved.

She broke the kiss and slowly slid her tongue down his body, leaving a trail of tingles that made him rock hard. Her hands gripped him, and then she placed her mouth over him, curling his toes, her mouth lavished him, sucking and pulling. Like a god, she worshipped him, causing his breathing to increase as his pulse began that steady beat towards completion.

Lovingly she caressed him, pushing him closer and closer to a climax. He ran his hands through her auburn hair, gripping her skull feeling her silken strands fall through his fingertips like sand.

A moan escaped him as he lay back against the pillows enjoying the feel of her mouth as she sucked him. This was paradise this was heaven. And if she didn't stop, she would finish him off.

Gently, he lifted her head and pulled her up beside him. His mouth moved over hers as he kissed her thoroughly. Breaking away, she gasped for air, her hands holding his head, grasping him. "I wanted to return the favor."

"And you did. But I can't wait to be inside you." Reaching into the nightstand he found a condom and slipped it on, knowing they weren't ready for a child.

Rolling her onto her back, he slid his body over hers, and without waiting, plunged inside her. She was like a balm that soothed his soul. When he was with Kelsey, even though there was a big black hole in his memory, it didn't seem to matter. He didn't feel anxious or worried that something would sneak up on him. Just the chance for them to make this life work.

Wrapping her arms around him, she whispered against his neck. "I don't want you to ever leave me again. I want you here beside me each night, filling me."

"Oh, Kelsey," he moaned, pulling out slowly and then ramming forward, wanting to brand his heart and his soul with the touch of her skin against his, knowing her request was impossible.

"Tyler," she cried as he felt her muscles clench him, grasping him clear to his heart, squeezing him as her fingers gripped the sheets, her back arching.

Quickly, he reached his own orgasm, clasping her to him. This was all he ever wanted or needed, Kelsey by his side with or without his memory.

A part of him cringed at the idea of never knowing what had happened those months he was deployed. Okay, so maybe he really did want to know what happened. But still he felt confident everything would come rushing back like a tidal wave when the timing was right. And then the U.S. Government would return him to the job he loved.

Chapter Six

Kelsey glanced at Tyler at her aunt's Christmas party. Standing next to the fireplace in his dress slacks, his red sweater, he fit in with her rambunctious family.

"Merry Christmas," her aunt called out handing out her holiday punch restricted to twenty-one and older. The recipe was known for encouraging people to shed their clothes. And Kelsey avoided the crazy drink. She watched as Tyler declined a glass her aunt offered.

He'd returned home a changed man. Even though she'd never expected to see him again, there were subtle differences in him. Now he was more withdrawn. Before he'd enjoyed parties, but not now. He almost acted guilty for being here, like he owed that damn war another chance at killing him.

And she had. She had almost lost him. The very thought was enough to bring tears to her eyes. Not only had she recklessly, selfishly dumped him via the U.S. Postal system, instead of waiting until he arrived home, she'd told him she couldn't live with him being gone. But an IUD had almost taken him from her forever. The U.S. government took him away most of the time, but the enemy had almost gotten him forever.

"Tyler, great to see you," her dad called rushing up to the man she loved. The man her father had told her she was nuts for dumping. He'd been right and that hurt even more.

He stood talking to her father and she watched as they walked away from the crowd. Hopefully her dad wouldn't be the one to tell him the truth. They had their heads bowed together, talking softly. Finally, her father smiled and nodded his head and then he clapped him on the shoulder and shook his hand. Whatever they were talking about must have been good. They wouldn't be laughing and smiling if he'd told Tyler about her moment of weakness.

Her sister walked to her side. "Have you told him yet?"

"Is he speaking to me?

"Yes."

"Then I haven't told him."

She shook her head at her.

Last night, she'd almost told him, but then he started kissing her and after that, there was no opportunity. They'd been busy showing how much they loved one another. "I'm waiting until after Christmas and then maybe I'll tell him."

"Aren't you worried that someone will tell him at the wedding?"

She grimaced and glanced at Tyler. "Of course I am. Joe almost let it slip the other night. Told Tyler he was going to ask me out, but since he saw us together, he decided not to. Like I would ever consider going out with him."

Even at this very second she was frightened that someone would confess to Tyler how weak she'd been. And the thought of him leaving again, terrified her. What if he were hurt again?

"I have a really bad feeling about this. You just need to be honest with him," Sara said, her eyes wide, her tone strict.

"I know. You've told me. I'll do it when the time is right, but not before." But when would that be? Right now he just seemed so vulnerable and she didn't want to make his misery any worse. She just didn't.

Yesterday, he'd mentioned the leadership qualities of a marine and she'd missed out on so many of them. She'd been weak and selfish, and a marine wife needed qualities that helped her man, not left him focusing on troubles at home when he was dodging bullets. She had failed miserably instead of being a helpmate to him, she'd been a drain.

"The wedding is in two days."

"So is Christmas."

Sara sighed. "Do you still love him?"

"More than ever."

Somehow she had to put aside her fears and make this man the best marine he could become. Even if that meant sacrificing her own needs.

"Then be honest with him. He'll take it better if he hears from you, not-"

"Shut up here he comes."

They stood there awkwardly, not saying a word, staring at one another when Tyler walked up. He glanced between the two of them. "Now this is a shock. You two are usually talking like two magpies."

They both started to say something at once. Finally, Sara turned to Kelsey. "You explain."

"We're arguing over which piece of borrowed jewelry she should wear. My grandmother's brooch or my mother's diamond necklace. Both pieces mean so much."

He laughed. "Wear them both."

Sara nodded her head. "Great suggestion. I think I will."

"Are you about ready to go?" Tyler asked.

Somehow she knew he'd reached his limit of people and it was time to leave. Since he'd come home her party boy no longer liked to be around large crowds. He preferred smaller groups and right now she would give him what he needed.

"Yes, I think so." Kelsey was tired and couldn't wait to get Tyler out of here before one of her family members slipped and said something that revealed her weakness.

"Good. See you at the wedding Sara," Tyler called, taking Kelsey's elbow.

"Yes, rehearsal tomorrow night."

"It's still not too late to change your mind."

"I would be dishonest," she said, looking pointedly at Kelsey, "if I said I hadn't considered it. But I love Jared too much and want to begin our relationship. With no secrets between us."

Tyler nodded and began to lead Kelsey towards the door. "See you tomorrow."

If it wasn't two days before her sister's big day, Kelsey would have killed her. As it was she wanted to yell and scream at her, but she just smiled. Guilt ate at her for being dishonest, but he didn't deserve the pain, the knowledge her letter would bring. After the wedding and Christmas, then she would tell him.

Tyler shook his head. "Sleep well."

~

When they reached her car, Tyler slid behind the wheel. "Your sister was acting strange."

"Yeah, I think she had pre-wedding jitters."

Sara was fine with the wedding, it was Kelsey's lack of honesty but she wasn't about to admit that to the man she loved. Not now.

He turned and smiled at her. "Would you have pre-wedding jitters?"

"No, I don't think so."

He patted her on the leg as he pulled out onto the highway that would take them back to her little house.

"What were you and my dad talking about?" she questioned.

He shrugged. "He was just telling me he was glad to see me and hoped I didn't have to go back."

"Will you have to return?" she asked, unable to stop herself. She'd tried very hard not to ask that question, but she couldn't keep the words from slipping out. She wanted to be strong for him. She wanted to show Tyler she could be a supportive marine wife.

She would have his back, regardless of her own wants and needs. And one moment she felt strong, then the next fear would consume her at the thought of him leaving again.

She was frightened, but leadership required courage and she was digging deep in her.

"I don't know. If my memory doesn't return, they may put me behind a desk until my enlistment is up. I'm not any good to them in black ops if I can't remember."

There was a moment of silence as she swallowed her anxiety, determined to be supportive. "What's the prognosis on your regaining your memory."

If he wanted to return to battle, then he needed his memory. She hated it, but she had to be honest with him. He needed the truth.

"They told me there is nothing stopping me from remembering. It could come back at any time. I wake up every morning hoping today is that day."

She gulped back the sob. She had to tell him. The sooner the better, before his memory returned.

"Tyler, I need to tell you something."

"What, honey?"

A loud bang exploded from the in front of the car and she watched in horror as Tyler jerked the wheel, the car turning sideways. He struggled to keep control of the car as he applied the brake.

"Tyler," she screamed as her car lurched and they spun on the road, the sound of the tire thumping loudly. After what felt like forever, but only a minute, the car came to a stop.

She glanced at him in the darkness. In the glow of the dash lights, she could see him shaking, his hands tightly gripped the wheel, his face ashen.

"Are you okay," she asked softly, shaking, wondering if the blowout had brought on another episode of PTSD.

Putting the car in park, he released his seat belt, opened the door and stepped out. She realized he was not responding to her question. He seemed to be in another world.

"Tyler," she cried.

He didn't say a word and she worried he'd slipped back into Afghanistan. She jumped out of the car and hurried after him. Snow pelted her, stinging her face, but she didn't feel the flakes. The cold seeped into her bones, making her shake even more.

Tyler stood staring at the car like he wanted to murder the shredded tire. Warning tingles spread through her as she watched him. This wasn't PTSD. This was something else.

"Are you all right," she said, gazing at him as snow pelted the two of them.

"I'm fine," he said brusquely. "Get back in the car."

His hands were shaking as he looked at the damage.

"Something's wrong," she said, staring at him, his body stiff, almost jerky, knowing instinctively there had been a shift in him.

He glanced up at her, his eyes blazing with rage. "Everything is just fine. The blow out brought back my memory. I remember everything."

Fear formed icicles around her heart. Trouble had ridden in on a blowout.

Chapter Seven

The car ride home was deafening, the silence so heavy, her ears ached from wanting him to say something, anything. Yell, scream at her, tell her she was a cold, selfish calculating bitch. But he said nothing.

When they reached the house, he waited for her to unlock the door. He walked into the house and stalked to the bedroom. She waited in the living room, pacing, when she heard him pull out his duffle bag.

She all but ran into the bedroom, halting at the doorway when she saw him stuffing his clothes into the bag.

"What are you doing?"

"I'm leaving. I remember the letter."

Fear froze her lungs, making it almost impossible to breathe. She had to make him see reason. She had to make him understand.

"No, Tyler, please listen to me. I made a huge mistake."

He wouldn't even look at her. He just kept stuffing that damn bag.

"Now, it's all coming together. Now, I understand why Joe wanted to ask you out. Why Mike thought that we split up. Now, I remember what a colossal bitch you are."

Her hand came up to her mouth trying to stifle the sob that threatened to choke her. "I was wrong."

How could she make him understand? She'd gotten scared. She'd had doubts about the life he wanted to live and her ability to handle his being gone.

"You're damn right you were."

"When I answered the door, you were standing in front of me with a bandage on your head. That grin that I could never refuse. I wanted you back. I'd missed you so much. I couldn't tell you the truth."

He continued jamming his clothes into the bag. "Do you know how much that letter hurt me? To think that you couldn't wait for me, tore me up inside."

She walked around to the bed and touched his arm, trying to soothe him, stop him. If he left, she feared he would never forgive her. "Stop! Please, look at me."

He jerked away from her touch and she felt a tear slide down her cheek. This couldn't be happening.

Finally, he glanced over at her. His blue eyes were gray ice and as cold as the storm raging outside. "I made a mistake. While you were strong, I was a coward and then one day, I just thought I can't do this anymore. If you were to get hurt or injured or even worse, I would die right alongside you."

She was slowly dying right now. How could it be any different and if he walked out the door what would she do?

"And do you think life with me is different now?"

"No. But I've changed. I'm stronger. I think now I can deal with you being gone."

That was only partly correct. She still had doubts about how she would handle him being away in a foreign land risking his life, but somehow she would find a way. She had to or lose him forever.

He went into the bathroom and grabbed his toiletries, shoving them into his bag. "I told you when I met you, that this was my life."

"And I thought I could deal with it. But it's harder than anything I've ever done. I missed you so much."

"So much you decided to end it with me." He zipped up his duffle bag, then lifted his head and gazed at her. "So tell me. Did you date anyone else? Did you sleep with anyone?"

"I had three single dates where I continuously compared them to you. And no, I never slept with anyone else. In fact, I was going to try to talk to you when you came home."

Those men were nothing. They were a total waste of her time. She should never have gone out, but she'd been lonely.

He lifted his duffle bag and threw it over his shoulder. "I texted Jared after I changed the flat. He's on his way to pick me up."

"No, I don't want you to leave. We need to talk this out."

He walked towards the door. She grabbed him by the arm. "Please, stay."

Gazing down at her, he just stared, his eyes colder than the arctic. "I'm not supposed to be here. You dumped me."

Tears filled her throat and a sob escaped. "I'm sorry. You were hurt, I missed you. I thought I was being given a second chance. I took it."

Headlights flashed in the driveway. "There's Jared."

"Tyler," she cried.

"You've had months to get over us. It's only been a few minutes for me. I need some space."

"No—" she cried.

He turned on his heel in that military strut that sent fury exploding inside her. The man wasn't going to let her explain, he wasn't going to sit down and talk about this rationally.

Oh no, he was going to walk out of there like the damn marine he was, which made her want to throw something at his back.

She watched as he walked out the door, leaving her life the same way he'd come in it, with her heart reeling, her emotions wrecked. Hanging her head, she knew she'd just lost everything.

~

Tyler was fighting mad. So much that he had Jared drop him off at the gym. He needed to express his fury in a positive way or someone would have a broken nose or a room destroyed. Releasing his hurt and frustration in the gym was so much safer. So he went several rounds with the punching bag, until his knuckles were bruised and bleeding. Still anger pervaded him like melt-off after a heavy snow.

The memory of the explosion was difficult, but her letter had seared his heart like a scared piece of meat. She'd given up on learning to live like a military wife. She'd given up not long after he'd been deployed.

And that's what hurt the most. The first time she felt fear for his safety, when she'd realized how dangerous his job really was, she'd decided this life wasn't for her. And maybe it wasn't for everyone, but he'd believed she was made of stronger stuff than to be such a coward.

Maybe everything she'd said was true. Maybe she'd made a mistake. Maybe she'd regretted her actions, but nothing had changed. He was still a soldier. He would be returning to Afghanistan or wherever the military sent him. And no matter what, his life would be in danger once again.

His chest ached, along with his hands. Regardless of what had happened tonight, he still loved Kelsey. But he needed some distance. He needed a chance to decide what his next step would be. Could he ever forgive her?

Grabbing his bag, he walked out of the gym. Jared leaned against his car. "Feel better?"

"No, but now I'm tired. I think I can sleep."

"I'm sorry, I didn't tell you. Sara kept saying we needed to stay out of it. And I went along with her, though she did encourage Kelsey to be honest with you."

"Thanks," he said wearily. "I feel like a fool."

Jared shook his head. "No, man. You didn't know."

"Funny thing is that I spoke to her father tonight to see what he thought about us getting married before I was sent away again." He shook his head, his skull throbbing. "That's not happening."

Last night when he couldn't sleep, he'd thought that maybe since Kelsey didn't want a big wedding, they could do their vows at midnight after her sister's big day. He didn't want to intrude on Jared and Sara's wedding, but he thought that maybe afterwards he and Kelsey could say their vows. But now, he didn't know what he wanted. Just get through tonight.

Jared shrugged his shoulders. "Sorry this all had to happen right here before Christmas and the wedding. Do you want to back out of the wedding."

Tyler glanced over at his friend. There was no way he could let him down, even under the most painful of situations, he would face Kelsey. He would show her what real courage looked like. "Absolutely not. I'm not letting her ruin your big event."

"Thanks, man. You know I had hoped you and Kelsey could work things out and we'd be brothers-in-laws."

"Me, too," Tyler said, his chest aching at the thought of Kelsey. She'd lied to him, she'd broken up with him and now her written words flashed across his brain like a teleprompter. Maybe it was time to move on.

"Are you certain you can't forgive her? You two have loved each other for a long time."

"Right now, it's like reliving her letter all over again. I need some time and some space. It's like being hurt a second time. The first one was tough, but the second time is devastating. Right now, I'm not ready to think of forgiving her. Why she lied, I don't understand. Nothing has changed."

Jared nodded. "I know. You're still a marine."

"So if she couldn't accept it before, why does she think it will be any different? It's just best if I end it now once and for all. Because there is no way she is ever going to accept being a military wife."

"I wish it was different," Jared said, "but fear you're right."

"I thought she'd be okay once I'd deployed, but obviously she couldn't handle my being gone. Nothing has changed. I'm still in the military. I'm still in danger and I'm not giving it up."

He loved his job, it was what defined him as a man. If he gave up the marines, he would slowly die. Which was worse? Losing Kelsey or his enlistment? He loved Kelsey, but being a soldier was his life. He didn't know how he could do without either one. It was killing him.

"Then it's time to move on."

Even the words seemed to rattle through Tyler's body like a snake issuing a warning, causing his stomach to clench. He'd loved Kelsey so much. For a moment he doubted his decision. He didn't want to live without her.

~

Kelsey was doing her best to act excited for her sister's wedding rehearsal. It wasn't fair to show how much she was broken inside after Tyler stormed out last night. The memory brought tears and she quickly composed herself.

They were at the church rehearsing the wedding and afterwards they were going to a catered dinner at Jared's family restaurant. They owned one of the largest steak houses in Denver and tonight they would celebrate the wedding of their son and Sara, while inside Kelsey slowly died.

"Okay, ladies, I want you to walk slowly down the aisle, turn and walk up onto the podium, turn and wait for the bride," the wedding consultant advised.

Kelsey was waiting her turn to go down the aisle, when she turned and faced her sister. She wanted to make certain she was ready for this wedding. That she had no doubts. She didn't want her sister to experience the kind of pain she was dealing with.

"Are you one hundred percent certain about this? I mean, it's not too late to turn back."

Sara glanced at her like she was crazy. "I've waited months to marry this man. What makes you think I want to back out?"

"I just want you to be happy." And she did. She hoped they had a long life together, filled with children and happiness.

More than anything, she wanted tonight and tomorrow to be focused on Sara and Jared. This was their moment in the sun, the beginning of their life together and she didn't want anything to mar this occasion.

"And I am. I think you're the one who's not certain," her sister whispered. "You're trying to put your problems on me."

"No, I'm not. I just don't want you to have any doubts."

Sara shook her head. "I told you this was going to backfire."

The wedding coordinator glanced at Kelsey. "Are you going to take your turn?"

"Oh, sorry," she said, as she turned and walked slowly down the aisle, unable to keep from noticing Tyler standing at the front beside Jared, watching her, his arctic blue eyes colder than the snow storm blowing outside.

A few minutes later, after everyone had practiced their parts, they had the attendants file out together. Tyler held out his arm to her as she was his attendant to escort back to the vestibule of the church.

"I tried to call you today," Kelsey whispered. "I want to talk to you."

"There's nothing left to say."

"You're not giving me a chance to explain."

"And you explained everything six months ago when you dumped me."

They reached the end of the aisle and he immediately dropped her arm and walked away, taking a piece of her heart with him. She wanted to run after and pull him to the side, but knew that would draw attention and she was doing her best not to ruin her sister's wedding. So she stood awkwardly off to the side with the other bridesmaids.

"Hey, Kelsey," Chris, one of the bridesmaids whispered. "I hear you and Tyler are back together again."

The woman was a man eating tiger who used men and there was no way Kelsey would stand back and let her have a go at her soldier. "We're working on resolving our issues."

It wasn't a complete lie. Though currently they were further apart than the Grand Canyon.

"Well, he certainly didn't look happy a minute ago. You guys have a fight?"

"We're concentrating on the wedding and the holidays. It's kind of a stressful time of year."

Tomorrow was Christmas Eve and Sara's wedding. And tonight, she had to somehow reconcile with Tyler. She just had to. They were meant to be together. She felt it and knew she'd screwed everything up. Somehow she had to make the hurt she'd caused right.

"Come on, ladies, I'm suppose, to make certain all of you are taken to the restaurant," Kelsey said, wishing she could skip this dinner, knowing instinctively, it was going to be a long punishing night.

For the next two hours she listened patiently to the speeches by family members, Tyler's toast and even her own father's teary breakdown at the idea of one of his daughters tying the knot. She was happy for Sara, but she wanted the evening to end so Kelsey could have a another chance to speak with Tyler.

Somehow she had to convince him to talk to her in private.

Just as the dinner ended, and everyone was saying goodbye, she watched as he excused himself to leave.

She hurried after Tyler, following him out the door. "Tyler, wait."

He turned and glared at her. "No Kelsey, we're not doing this. I'm not going to talk to you right now."

"Why?" she asked. "Why won't you give me a chance to explain?"

"You explained yourself pretty damn well in the letter you sent. And I've gotten to relive this heartache more than once. This is the second time I've gone through this agony. Now, excuse me while I leave."

"But, Tyler-"

"Good night, Kelsey."

It was late, she should give up and call it a night. She watched as he hurried across the sidewalk and opened the door to a car she didn't recognize. He climbed behind the wheel and backed out of the parking space. He pulled out onto the road.

She was just about to turn away and return inside, when she saw a dark car weaving across the road, barreling towards Tyler on the wrong side of the highway. In horror, she watched the sedan slam into Tyler's Honda, catching the edge of the car and sending it flying through the air.

With a loud crash the vehicle flipped and then slammed into the ground on its roof sliding across the road, where it spun for several moments.

The screech of metal and plastic parts went flying across the road.

Her heart slammed inside her chest, her feet moving automatically as she ran. Screaming reached her ears and she realized the sound came from her mouth. She hurried to reach the man she loved. Her fingers automatically dialed 911.

"Tyler," she cried as she reached his car. "Dear God, please don't be dead."

Chapter Eight

Tyler felt an incredible sense of *déjà vu* sweep over him and for a moment his mind tried to travel back to Afghanistan. Only this time he was hanging upside down in his rental car. Shaking his head, he tried to clear the fog that wanted to settle over his mind.

"Tyler!" He heard Kelsey screaming. "Are you all right."

The sound of guns firing resounded in his head and then he heard her sweet voice and he suddenly was grounded in the here and now.

She knelt in the snow, gazing through the window at him. "Dear God, tell me you're okay."

How did he know if he was truly all right? He'd just been flipped through the air. A slow throb was beginning in his temple, but he'd just rolled his car, what more could he expect.

"I think so."

His head and neck were aching all ready and he knew that by tomorrow he would be sore. The car had been on the wrong side of the road without his lights on. Tyler hadn't had a chance.

"Paramedics are on their way," she said.

He tried to crawl out and realized he was pinned in the car. "I can't move."

"Don't," she demanded. "Let them get you out."

The world swam before him and he felt darkness closing in around him. Then an incredible urge to throw up had him fighting nausea. He felt a trickle of blood run down his forehead. Damn, he couldn't seem to keep his brains from being hit.

She reached into the car and handed him a tissue. "Press this against your head."

Sirens blared through the night and he realized they were coming to him. "I don't want this to ruin Sara and Jared's wedding."

She ignored him. "Where are you hurt?"

Tyler had no idea. Right now he just ached and wanted to stay here listening to Kelsey's voice and not slip back into Afghanistan.

"I'm okay. I'd feel better if I could get out of this car."

Why was it, she seemed to see him at his weakest, when all he wanted was to appear strong to this woman he loved. Yet, she'd hurt him so badly that he needed to put space between them. He had to learn to live without her. "You don't have to wait. I'm okay."

He feared he was going to throw up and didn't want her to see him.

"I'm not going anywhere."

"Just leave," he said, in a demanding voice, not wanting her to see him in this state. He didn't know what was wrong, but he knew he was going to soon throw up. It was only a matter of time.

An ambulance pulled up in front of the two vehicles, their lights flashing, radiating through the car. Kelsey jumped up and he heard her calling to them, but by this time he felt like he was going to pass out.

"Here, he's in here."

A man gazed in at him. "Hi, sir. Tell me your name."

"Tyler Ferguson."

"Any allergies to medicine?"

"No."

The paramedic checked the car, trying to find a way to release Tyler, but his legs were trapped.

"Okay, we're going to get the jaws of life and get you out of there. Are you hurting anywhere?"

Tyler sighed and gazed at the man. "I'm pretty nauseous."

"That's normal. It's a reaction to shock. Can you move your toes? Your fingers?" the paramedic asked.

"Everything works."

"Great. Let's get you out of there," he walked away.

Kelsey leaned back down to the car. "I'm right here, I haven't left. The firemen are walking over. You stay strong, Tyler. I love you."

Her words calmed him and his chest ached with the need to tell her he loved her, but he wasn't ready to confess his feelings again. He needed more time.

"Go home, Kelsey. The paramedics are here."

If she stayed he feared he'd give into her.

"Not on your life. I'll see you at the hospital."

She disappeared from the window. Her being here confused him even more, but left a warm feeling in his chest that she hadn't deserted him. She could have.

Jared stuck his head in the window. "Hey, man, you okay?"

"Honestly, I don't know. Try to get Kelsey to go home."

"Will do. They're coming with the jaws of life. Hang in there."

A few seconds later, he heard Jared yell at Kelsey. "Go home with your sister. You're not needed here."

"You may soon be my brother-in-law, but that doesn't give you the right to tell me what to do. I'm not leaving. You can't make me."

"No, but I can ask you to go. He doesn't want you here," Jared said.

Tyler didn't know what he wanted. His feelings for Kelsey were so mixed up. He loved and he hated Kelsey, but he didn't want her to leave him. He missed the feel of her hand on him.

Fog seemed to settle over his brain and he could hear them arguing in the distance, but didn't have the energy to call to them.

Just then he heard the paramedic yell, "Get a move on, we need to get him out of here. He's losing consciousness."

The world went black.

~

Kelsey sat in the waiting area of the hospital. It was past two in the morning and she was exhausted, but she wasn't leaving. Tyler was still in the ER and they had not given her any information.

Jared had left an hour ago, but she sat waiting anxiously. She refused to go home until Tyler was in a room and told her to leave. Then she would probably give in. But right now, she was here to stay.

Finally, the ER doc came out of the emergency room and smiled at her. "Are you family?"

"I'm his fiancée."

She wasn't willing to give up that title just yet.

"From the description of the crash, Mr. Ferguson is an extremely lucky young man. He has a pretty bad concussion. The night is almost over, but I'd like him to remain here at least until in the morning. That way we can monitor him for any other injuries. They just moved Mr. Ferguson to room 304."

"What about the wedding tomorrow?"

"If he feels up to it, then I say yes, but no drinking, no driving. I'd really like him to take it easy for the next week."

"Thank you," she said, jumping up.

She hurried toward the elevator and rode up to the third floor. When the elevator dinged, she all but ran to his room. When she reached the door, she hesitated. He was sound asleep.

His face was pale and now he had suture tape over his brow where he'd hit his head on the steering wheel. Her heart clenched at the sight of him. He looked so fragile and there was no way she could walk away tonight. He might need her.

Quietly, she slipped into the room, sat down in the chair and pulled her coat up for cover. She would sleep here and then return home in the morning in time to get ready for the wedding.

Watching him sleep, she realized how close she'd come to losing him tonight. He could have been so easily killed by that drunk driver. If his car had been farther in the intersection, they'd be talking about a funeral tomorrow instead of a wedding.

Staring at his dark hair that draped across his forehead, the force of her love hit her chest like an explosion, almost knocking the breath from her.

His happiness was more important than anything and if being in the military was what he desired, then she would have to make the necessary adjustments to give her man what he needed.

Sure she had needs and he'd always been thoughtful to make certain her desires were fulfilled, but this was one time, she had to concede and give him what he demanded if she wanted to be with Tyler. And she did. She wanted him more than she wanted her next breath.

She would never enjoy him being a marine, but with time, she would learn to live this life.

The wreck had made her realize that she could lose him anytime, anywhere. It didn't matter that he loved the marines and was in a foreign country doing dangerous work, he could just as easily be killed here. And she knew she had to show him that no matter what happened or where, she would always be there for him.

She might have to miss her sister's wedding, because she was not leaving his side until he awoke.

Reaching out she stroked a piece of his dark hair away from his face. She didn't know how to prove to him how much she loved him. All she knew was that she would be here when he awoke in the morning.

"Sleep well, my love," she whispered and kissed him on the cheek. "I'll be right here beside you tonight."

~

Tyler woke early the next morning, his head pounding. The first thing he saw was Kelsey, curled up in a chair, her coat wrapped around her.

He was sore, thirsty, and had a headache.

But the sight of Kelsey filled him with both hope and anger. Why did she write him that Dear John letter if she cared as much as she said? Was it a moment of weakness and if so, would she give up the next time he was deployed?

He didn't want to be here when she woke. Reaching over he turned the IV machine off, ripped the tape off and pulled the needle out of his arm. Being in a hospital for several weeks you learned the routine.

Slipping out of bed, for a moment he felt a wave of dizziness. They had told him last night they wanted to keep him for observation. Well the night was over, he was fine and he'd had enough of hospitals to last him a lifetime.

Quickly he found his clothes. Using his training, he quietly slipped them on, carrying his shoes out the door. He approached the nurse's desk.

"I'm checking out."

She glanced up at him, her eyes, giving him that I don't need this kind of crap today. "You pulled your IV out. Let me see your arm."

He gave her is arm. "It's fine."

She shook her head at him "I'm the nurse. You're the patient. You should crawl back in bed and wait until the doctor examines you."

"I'm going, I've got a wedding to attend."

"To that sweet young girl in your room?"

"No, her sister's wedding," he said. "My friend Jared is marrying her sister."

"You had a car accident. You're not leaving here without me checking your vitals."

"If I let you check my vitals, will you give me paperwork to get out of here."

"You'll have to sign a release form stating you left without medical approval." The woman stared at him and shook her head. "I better not catch any crap from the doctor about this or I will hunt you down."

He grinned. "I spent two weeks in a hospital in Germany. I don't want to be here."

The nurse nodded. "Yeah, your girlfriend told the doctor. Now, sit down and let me check your blood pressure and put some tape on your arm."

"Oh, and would you let her sleep as long as possible."

"Do you think this is a hotel?"

"Hell no, but she needs the rest."

Shaking her head, the nurse sighed. "I'll do what I can."

Tyler didn't want to have to deal with her disappointment and frustration. He just knew that at this moment, he'd made up his mind. He was leaving.

The nurse shook her head at him. "If I were her, I'd be so upset with you, sneaking out and not waking me after I waited all night."

"You're right. She's going to be mad."

But he wasn't ready to talk with her. Talking should be done at the right time. Not before her sister's wedding, with them both anxious was not the time.

Vaguely he remembered her kissing him goodnight. She hadn't stopped loving him. She'd just grown frightened and weak.

He glanced at his watch. The wedding was in six hours. He had to pick up his tux, get another rental car and get some rest before the start of tonight's events. The wedding would be the event of the year, possibly of his life.

Chapter Nine

Tyler sat in the groom's room, waiting for the wedding to begin. His body ached from the crash and he knew the throbbing headache was a result of the concussion he'd suffered.

Kelsey hadn't called or tried to see him since he'd left the hospital and that was good. He still felt confused and didn't know what to do. He loved her, but sending him the worst letter a soldier could receive was just above cheating.

He'd watched men go almost crazy, unable to talk to their woman when they were so far from home. It was a soldier's worst nightmare and he'd been so lucky he got to live through it not once, but twice.

Yet, she had tried to make it up to him when he'd been injured. But would she do this again as soon as he left?

There was a knock on the door.

"She's backing out," Mike, one of the groomsmen, teased.

"Not funny," Jared replied as he was slipping into his tux, getting ready to take pictures.

"Hey, it's for Tyler," the same groomsmen said glancing over to where Tyler was sitting.

He looked up. "What?"

"It's a love letter for you," Mike said, handing him the sealed envelope.

Tyler walked away from everyone and opened the envelope.

Dear Tyler,

I was wrong to send you a Dear John letter and regretted it almost the moment I dropped it into the mailbox. What can I say? I got weak. I became a news junkie sitting in front of the television looking for anything about Afghanistan. I couldn't sleep at night because I worried you were sitting in some terrorist jail about to be beheaded. I stopped eating because I was so afraid of seeing a chaplain walk up to my door to deliver the bad news.

You are my first experience with the military. I didn't grow up seeing my father leave and go away for months at a time. I never realized the hardships that military families deal with every day. Now, I understand and respect the wives who live without their husbands. Coping with children and all of life's stresses without their man by their side.

When you arrived on my doorstep injured, there was no way I could turn you away and by this time I knew I'd made the biggest mistake of my life. My plan had been to contact you when you came home and beg you to take me back and give me a second chance. With your memory loss, I thought I had another opportunity to make right the terrible mistake I'd made.

Watching that car slam into yours the other night, I realized I could lose you at any time and the hurt would be the same. I could lose you today, or when we're seventy-five and regardless it's going to be traumatic.

I know I don't deserve another opportunity with you, but if you are willing to try again, I will do everything I can to learn to accept being a military wife. I will keep the home fires burning, raise our children and make a place where you can come home and rest. I'll join with the other military wives and support you any way that I can.

I love you, Tyler, and I know I screwed up. Consider this the reverse Dear John letter. Consider this letter the one where I ask you to give us another chance.

Love,

Kelsey

For a moment, Tyler just stood and let her words wash over him. He still loved her. He knew he wanted to give them a second chance.

Last night she'd shown him that she really did care. Maybe she had made a mistake. Not seeing that car with no lights on had been a mistake that almost cost him his life. It had killed the drunken driver. Maybe he should forgive Kelsey?

Life was precious and it didn't matter if he was in the States or out, he could go at any second. They were wasting precious time arguing. But could she live with him in the military?

Since he'd returned home she'd been nothing but caring. She said she'd had a weak moment. Didn't they all suffer from weak moments? If she was willing to give them a second chance with the knowledge that he would retire from the military, then he wanted to try again.

But this time before he left, she would be acquainted with several military wives. Women who would help her deal with the loneliness, the anxiety of him being gone. A support system to help her live with the day-to-day fear of being married to a soldier. People who would be there for her if the worst happened to him. Marine sisters.

His heart knew what he wanted to do, but the logical, clear-thinking marine wasn't certain she could handle his life. But his heart was telling him don't be a fool.

~

Kelsey walked down the aisle of the church toward the preacher, her new brother-in-law and Tyler. All she could see was her soldier man, waiting at the front of the church, his arctic blue eyes gazed at her as she came toward the group of men.

She had awakened this morning to an empty hospital bed. They were still right where they'd left off two days ago.

The nurse told her he'd left instructions for her not to be awakened and she'd been angry when she realized she'd slept so soundly that he'd been able to leave.

Though her heart was bruised, battered and aching worse than a heart attack, she couldn't help but think after tonight, she would slink away and never see Tyler again. How could she blame him, she'd never forgive herself either.

He wasn't going to exonerate her and though she doubted she would ever recover, she had to put this behind her and move on. She'd made the biggest mistake of her life and now had to live with the repercussions of her decisions.

When she reached the podium, she turned and waited while the music changed and everyone stood for the bride. Tears clogged her throat as she watched her beautiful sister float down the aisle, a smile of happiness on her face, her green eyes filled with love for Jared. This was their big day and tonight their life together began. A life she wished she could have with Tyler, but it wasn't meant to happen. There had been no response to her letter.

Her throat clogged with tears as she watched Jared, smiling at her sister and knew he would do everything he could to make Sara happy.

For the next thirty minutes, she fought the emotions that threatened to spill at how much in love her sister and Jared were as they said their vows. Tyler wouldn't even meet her gaze. It was over. She knew it was over and that made this ceremony even more painful. She'd dreamed of staring at her man while her sister and Jared said their I do's, thinking of how it would be when she and Tyler were wed.

And now that would never happen. Never.

After the ceremony, and the thousands of pictures, the newlyweds went into the reception hall.

Kelsey took her sister's bridal bouquet from her and set it on the table. She was seated down from the bride and groom with Tyler being not more than two chairs from her.

Finally, unable to stand it any longer she turned to him. "Are you okay?"

"Yes," he responded and turned away, crushing her very soul. So this was how it was going to be.

Soon it was time for the toasts and Tyler clinked his glass and then stood waiting for everyone to get quiet.

"Jared, Sara, today is a special day. It's Christmas Eve and in about two hours, Santa is going arrive delivering holiday gifts for all the little boys and girls who've been nice this year." The crowd chuckled. "But you two. You've already received the best Christmas gift.

"You've received the gift of sharing forever with each other. From now until the time you each take your last breath, your Christmas will be spent with the memory of how you began your life together.

"May you always stand beside each other, never let doubt tear you apart. Always be strong and support of each other. May your life be richly blessed with happiness, babies, and continued love for one another." He raised his champagne glass. "Congratulations."

Everyone cheered and Tyler sat down. It was a simple, elegant toast that brought tears to Kelsey's eyes. Only two weeks ago, she'd thought she would never see him again and now here he was at her sister's wedding. And she was broken hearted.

It was her turn to toast the happy couple and she stood, confident in what she was about to say. "Jared and Sara, you've waited a long time for this day. But while you waited, I've seen the two of you change and grow.

"The sign of a good leader is knowing when a team member is weak, they must use their leadership skills to strengthen that person. The two of you have made mistakes along the way, but you've overcome obstacles and grown stronger.

"While you were weak, Jared was your strength When he became weak you became strong. You two have always been there, leaning on each other.

"Never let anything or anyone question what you feel for one another. Always continue to look to each other when you need strength. If all of us were as confident in love as the two of you, the world would be a better place. Congratulations."

Everyone cheered and raised their glasses. Kelsey sank down into her chair, wanting this wedding, this day of happiness for her sister to end as quickly as possible. So that she would never have to see the man whose heart she'd broken ever again. This wasn't a happy occasion for her and Tyler because of her own weakness. If only she'd remained strong, things would have been so different today.

When the dancing began, Kelsey waltzed with her father and then with several of the other groomsmen, but she refused to look to see what Tyler was doing. She had to put this behind her and the sooner the better.

Finally, towards the end of the night, the groomsmen gathered around for the tossing of the garter. Jared rounded up the single men and Tyler was right there in the midst. When Jared pulled up her sister's wedding dress, and slid the garter down, he shielded her leg from the other men's view.

"That's mine," he playfully called as he yanked her sister's wedding gown down, covering her and Kelsey smiled. Jared turned his back to the men and slung the garter belt over his shoulder. "Catch it."

Kelsey watched in horror as Tyler jumped in front of her cousin and grabbed it out of the air. "Got it."

Soon it was the single women's turn to catch the bridal bouquet and Kelsey knew she wanted no part of the action, she turned her back to walk away and her sister called out. "Kelsey where are you going. Get in here."

Reluctantly, she turned back toward the women to please her sister. It was after all Sara's big day and Kelsey didn't want to mar it with her attitude. And she definitely had an attitude when it came to love. She was done. Over it, though her heart kept telling her otherwise.

Sara turned her back and tossed the bouquet in the air. The women parted and Tyler reached out and grabbed it.

"Hey, you're not a single woman," one of the bridesmaids yelled.

"Sorry, I need that bouquet."

He grinned at her and walked over to where Kelsey was standing. He smiled at her the way he had in the past and her stomach rolled like a ship at sea. He dropped down on bended knee, took her hand in his.

She could feel her heart about to explode inside her chest.

"Kelsey Johnson I've loved you for a long time, but you've had your doubts. I know that my life is not easy, but last night you proved to me that I think you've changed and grown. You stood by me, when no one else would have. I may have lost my memory for a while, but I never got over my feelings for you. Will you marry me, tonight, right this moment? Will you be my wife?"

Kelsey stared at him. He loved her. "Have you forgiven me?"

"That's the past. Let's start over. I love you."

"Oh, Tyler, I never thought I'd hear those words again."

"Will you marry me?"

"Yes, of course I will."

The crowd around them cheered and she pulled him to his feet. Five minutes later, after they had received everyone's congratulations, she pulled him into an alcove.

She kissed him hard on the lips and then she pulled back and stared into his eyes. "So you're really no longer angry with me?"

"It's behind us. Your letter this morning made everything clear. By staying at the hospital with me, you showed me you can be a strong supporter. With my help, you'll become a strong marine's wife."

"And when I get weak?"

"I'll help you. And when I get scared and weak?"

"I'll be there for you."

He smiled at her. "Honey, I want to get married tonight."

"But we don't have a license."

"We'll get the legalities all taken care of after the holidays. But I think we should get married at the stroke of midnight and spend Christmas as newlyweds."

She smiled at him, her heart filling with love for her soldier. "I love that idea."

~

It was midnight. The bride and groom were standing beside Kelsey and Tyler, her parents were there and a few of the guests still at the wedding. The preacher, a family friend, had agreed to stay even though they knew the ceremony wasn't legal. They had no license, but wanted to say their vows in front of friends and family.

In the next day or two they would have a civil ceremony at the courthouse, but tonight was about celebrating their love for one another.

Kelsey glanced at Tyler and he smiled at her as he said his vows. They had agreed to wait until midnight – Christmas Day to say their I do's.

Love shone from Tyler's eyes as he promised to love her until death did they part.

When they were finished, the minister turned to them. "You may kiss your bride."

Tyler pulled her into his arms. "Losing my memory, brought me back to you, and I'll be forever grateful to that roadside bomb."

"And I'm thankful you came back. But let's not risk it again. I've accepted that there will be times your job takes you away from me, but please know I will be here waiting for you. Waiting on you to return to me."

"I love you, Kelsey."

"I love you, Tyler."

"I now present Mr. and Mrs. Tyler Ferguson."

Their family and friends surrounded them and Kelsey only wanted to get her marine home all to herself where they could celebrate their Christmas wedding properly.

Thank you for reading!

Dear Reader,

Thank you so much for reading *Her Christmas Lie*. I'd never written a military story before and have so much respect for the families of our military men and women. I just can't imagine not seeing your husband or wife for months at a time and constantly worrying about their safety. They all deserve so much respect for their sacrifice. If there are military errors, it's the writers fault. I did talk to several enlisted men, one who had me change the cover, thank you, Bruce.

Whether or not you loved the book or hated it, I would appreciate it if you let everyone know by leaving a few words on your favorite vendor's website.

If you enjoy western historical authors, please join the Pioneer Hearts group on Facebook. This is a fabulous group of readers and authors who enjoy westerns. We have lots of fun and there is always something going on.

Sign up for my newsletter if you'd like to learn about my new releases before everyone else.

Thanks for venturing into my world and I hope to see you here again soon.

Yours in Drama, Divas, Bad Boys and Romance!
Sincerely,

Sylvia McDaniel

Books by Sylvia McDaniel

Contemporary Romance

Standalones
The Reluctant Santa
My Sister's Boyfriend
The Wanted Bride
The Relationship Coach
Her Christmas Lie
Secrets, Lies, and Online Dating
Paying for the Past
Cupid's Revenge

Anthologies
Kisses, Laughter & Love
Christmas with you

Collaborative Series

Magic, New Mexico
Touch of Decadence

Western Historicals

Standalones
A Hero's Heart
A Scarlet Bride
Second Chance Cowboy

The Cuvier Women
Wronged
Betrayed
Beguiled

Lipstick and Lead
Desperate
Deadly
Dangerous
Daring
Determined
Deceived

Scandalous Suffragettes
Abigail
Bella
Callie
Faith

The Burnett Brides
The Rancher Takes a Bride
The Outlaw Takes a Bride
The Marshal Takes a Bride
The Christmas Bride

Anthologies
Wild Western Women
Courting the West
Wild Western Women Ride Again

Collaborative Series

The Surprise Brides
Ethan

American Mail Order Brides
Katie

About the Author

Sylvia McDaniel is a best-selling, award-winning author of historical romance and contemporary romance novels. Known for her sweet, funny, family-oriented romances, Sylvia is the author of The Burnett Brides, a western historical western series, The Cuvier Widows, a Louisiana historical series, and several short contemporary romances.

She is the former President of the Dallas Area Romance Authors, a member of the Romance Writers of America®, and a member of Novelists Inc. Her novel, A Hero's Heart, was a 1996 Golden Heart Finalist. Several other books have placed or won in the San Antonio Romance Authors Contest and the LERA Contest, and she was a Golden Network Finalist.

Married for nearly twenty years to her best friend, they

have two dachshunds that are beyond spoiled and a good-looking, grown son who thinks there's no place like home. She loves gardening, shopping, knitting, and football (Cowboys and Bronco's fan), but not necessarily in that order.

Look for her the first Tuesday of every month at the Plotting Princesses blogspot, and be sure to sign up for her newsletter to learn about new releases and contests. Every month a new subscriber is entered into a drawing for a free book!

She can be found online at: www.sylviamcdaniel.com or on Facebook. You can write to Sylvia at P.O. Box 2542, Coppell, TX 75019.

Sneak Peek into Cupid's Revenge

Entering the city limits of Cupid, Texas for the first time in ten years was like going to the dentist for a root canal. Painful and numbing. But Skye Brand wouldn't miss the Valentine Day wedding of her close friend, Michelle, though the event would be a happy occasion sprinkled with intermittent, agonizing remembrances of Zane Calhoun.

Michelle had informed her Zane was a groomsman in the wedding. Single and still hated Skye.

She glanced over in the car at her long-haired dachshund, Putz, who sat in his carrier, watching her drive. "It's just you and me, buddy. We don't need a man in our life."

Putz tilted his head and gazed at her with his beady brown eyes, trying to understand, gazing at her with unconditional love. Dogs were so easy compared to men. Food, water and love, and they were yours for life.

Skye stopped at the town's only stop light. A sign said High School State Football Champions and listed the years the local team reigned supreme in the state of Texas. Zane had played defensive end their senior year when they won State. The memory of that night felt like it happened yesterday. Yeap, this weekend would be like every dental nightmare all wrapped up in white wedding cake.

The town hadn't changed much in ten years. A new box store added at the edge of town, a fresh coat of paint on the local DQ and the cupid statue still sat in the town's square. What idiot thought a man in a diaper with a bow and arrow was cute?

She pulled up in front of The Cupid Love Nest, a bed and breakfast run by Mabel Underwood, who could spread secrets faster than the internet. A white Victorian two story home surrounded by a wrap-around porch adorned with rocking chairs was the town's only bed and breakfast. The house belonged in a different era and gazing at the older home Skye wondered what she was doing back in Cupid.

After waffling for months about whether or not to return for Michelle's wedding, Mabel's was the only place she'd been able to get a room. Michelle's large family had sold out the only decent hotel in town and Skye refused to stay at the Valentine Express where rooms were rented by the hour.

Skye parked the car, took Putz out of his carrier and put his leash on him. She grabbed her suitcase, the make-up bag that held the tools of her trade, and started up the steps.

A gray-haired Mabel met her at the door, her reading glasses tilted on the end of her nose. "I'm sorry, we're all booked up this weekend.

"I have a reservation."

Mabel frowned at the dog. "No pets."

"Mabel, its Skye Brand. I made a reservation a month ago and you sent me an email saying I could bring my dog."

"That girl from Cupid High School, whose parents were killed in that horrible crash out on highway 67?"

Skye tensed. Was the tragic death of her parents the only thing people remembered about her?

"Skye Brand, make-up artist and stylist. Former Valedictorian for the class of 2002," Skye said regretting she'd only received a thousand dollar scholarship for college.

"Well come on in, honey, I didn't recognize you with your hair all colored and frizzed like that," Mabel said, as she opened the door.

Skye's short hair had blonde tips and she'd put enough mouse in it to make her appear like she'd juiced up on electricity first thing this morning. According to Vogue the spiked look was the latest fashion. She'd wanted her return to reflect she was no longer that small town girl who'd left numb with grief and fear. She'd brought the latest big city hairdo home to Cupid.

She stepped over the threshold and entered the big house with Putz right behind her.

Mabel stared at her dachshund, her frame bent over. "He's had all his shots and he doesn't have fleas, does he?"

"All shots and no fleas."

"Okay," she said hesitation in her voice. "I need you to sign this paperwork. Breakfast is from seven thirty to nine. That's the only meal I provide. What brings you back to town?"

"Michelle Cooper's wedding. I'm doing her hair and make-up."

Mabel frowned at her. "I hope you don't intend to style her hair like yours. Maybe that's what those women in Dallas wear, but it needs a good combing."

"This is Michelle's day and I'll fix her hair however she wants," Skye said, wanting to tell Mabel her hair style was the latest fashion.

"Michelle's got good sense. She's marrying that Vanderbilt boy."

Skye didn't say anything. She'd been shocked when Michelle announced her engagement to Ryan. They just didn't seem to go together. But if that was who her friend chose to marry, she'd support her decision.

"I'm putting you in the Cupid Bow room, since you're not wearing a wedding ring and no man is with you. Maybe the ambiance of the room will help you find true love," Mabel said handing her the key.

Mabel hadn't changed. Still outspoken with little or no tact, a mouth the size of a megaphone with enough connections in town to blast gossip in minutes. Within the hour, Skye's return to Cupid would be all over town.

"Mabel, you're too kind," Skye said. But the sarcasm

was lost on the innkeeper.

"Keep your dog on a leash. My Scottie recently had surgery, so I'm trying to keep her quiet. She's getting old and grumpy."

Not unlike her owner, Skye thought. Maybe there was something to people looking and acting like their pets. She glanced down at Putz. Yep, the patch of long blonde hair on the top of his head stood straight up, matching her own.

"Your room's at the top of the stairs, two doors down and on the right."

"Thanks," Sky said, juggling her bags.

Skye carried her suitcase and makeup bag upstairs with Putz following obediently. Later, she would get his carrier and bring that up as well, but right now she just wanted to unpack, call Michelle, settle in and relax.

An hour later, she descended the stairs eager to take Putz for a well-deserved walk. She'd changed into her jogging outfit, her short spiky blonde hair still stood on end and she'd brushed a new coat of striking hot pink lipstick across her lips. Later tonight, the plans were to meet her girlfriends from school and catch up. Putz trailed down the stairs behind her. When they reached the entry way, she turned to her faithful dachshund.

"Do you wanna go for a walk?"

He danced around in circles, barking. She snapped the leash on his collar and he raced towards the door almost dragging her.

It was then she glanced up into the searing brown-eyed gaze she'd dreaded seeing. She froze, staring at how much he'd changed. How the boy had become a man and she almost quit breathing.

"Zane," she said, in a breathless rush, her body betraying her by reacting to the sight of the boy she'd once loved.